Memoirs

OF AN INVISIBLE WOMAN

Volume 1

REEM DENISE

Copyright © 2024 by Reem Denise

All rights reserved. No part of this book may be reproduced, distributed, or transmitted in any form or by any means, including photocopying, recording, or other electronic or mechanical methods, without the prior written permission of the author, except in the case of brief quotations embodied in critical reviews and certain other non-commercial uses permitted by copyright law.

Disclaimer: This book is inspired by true events. Some names, characters, and incidents have been changed to protect the privacy of individuals, and certain events have been fictionalized for dramatization.

I dedicate this book to my amazing children and grandchildren, who always push me to be my best, even when I didn't know my best! My children are such amazing adults, and I couldn't imagine walking this life without them. My grandchildren are my reason to keep going. I have to leave an inheritance for them. I want them to know to always do their best, and the sky is the limit for them. DootDoot loves you to the moon and back.

Table of Contents

Introduction 1

Chapter One 5

Chapter Two 21

Chapter Three 37

Chapter Four 47

Chapter Five 65

Chapter Six 81

Chapter Seven 91

Chapter Eight 99

Chapter Nine 111

Chapter Ten 121

Chapter Eleven 131

Chapter Twelve 141

Chapter Thirteen 151

Chapter Fourteen 159

Chapter Fifteen 173

Introduction

The problem with juggling two lives is eventually something falls. The woman staring back at me felt like a stranger and I wasn't sure how much longer I could pretend to know her.

I sat in my vanity surrounded by everything I built wondering why it still felt like something was missing. The weight of two worlds felt heavier than ever as I stared into my own tired eyes. I had everything I thought I wanted, so why did it feel like I was losing control?

Reem Denise

The woman in the mirror was successful, powerful, and exhausted I didn't know how to save her. I used to see such confidence when I looked in the mirror, now all I see are cracks. The reflection I looked at felt more like a mask than my face. Two lives, two identities, still no one truly knows me. I was tired of pretending to have it all together when everything felt like it was falling apart every time I looked in the mirror.

My vanity was covered in my makeup, jewelry, and lies. The makeup on my face could hide a lot but I was still so aware of the truth. Success had come easy, but peace felt impossible. No one tells you that having it all comes with a price, and I was running out of ways to pay.

So, I just stared at my reflection, looking for I don't know what – answers, encouragement, inspiration? Maybe a sign from above, telling me everything was going to be all right. My light-skinned brown face looked worn out and frustrated, a little sad. I sighed, closed my deep brown eyes, and rubbed my hands around my face and shoulders.

Memoirs of an Invisible Woman

My ways of getting things done in my life were a little unorthodox, but to me they were effective. I just wanted the best for my family. Always. But my love life was taking a toll on me, and I didn't know how much longer I could put up with the bullshit while taking care of everything and everyone else. I was a mother, daughter, sister, boss, and girlfriend in one world. I was an exotic dancer in another. I had beautiful children, crazy sex almost every day, and a head for business. There was a line of people wanting me to do their hair and another line of niggas wanting me to dance in their clubs. I loved the fact that I didn't have to ask anybody for anything, and I could provide for my kids the way I saw fit. There was no way I'd ever be broke. On the one hand, I loved my life. But on the other hand, I felt lost.

I put my arms down and looked back at the face in the mirror. It seemed a little familiar, but I didn't really know her anymore. How could I juggle all the components of two lives and still never have anyone see me for who I truly was? I had so much going for me, but there seemed to be a void in my life. All I ever wanted was to be loved unconditionally. But it was like I was flying through the air as a trapeze artist, wary of the dangerous fall, and no one was watching. I was performing amazing feats of courage, but no one noticed. I was invisible.

Chapter One

Where do I begin this story? Oh, yes—the day I met Julian. Let me tell you about him.

I was shoving popcorn into my mouth at a local basketball game with my sister, Mina. Her fat-ass husband, Hank—who I secretly called Humpty Dumpty—was playing. I could hear the squeak of tennis shoes on the hardwood floor and the coaches cussing at their players. The crowd was full of wives, girlfriends, co-workers, friends, and restless kids. Little boys and girls were chasing each other up and down the bleachers, while teenagers snuck away to meet by the lockers. Life in Cincinnati, Ohio, was all about family and sports.

Reem Denise

I laughed at Hank, running down the court, panting and sweaty. If you haven't guessed by now, I couldn't stand him. But Mina? She was my everything. She was two years older than me, but for some reason, people always thought we were twins—even though we looked nothing alike, in my opinion. Mina was thirty-six, about 5'2", and had a thick body like a video vixen. She always wore her shoulder-length hair in a stupid ponytail, never letting it down. I couldn't believe she was happy being such a Plain Jane. I'd tried to get her to dress more sensually, but she never budged. We were total opposites in that regard.

Mina and Hank had been married for about 15 years, and they had five kids, but you wouldn't know it by looking at her. She was a gym fanatic, always working out and taking it way too seriously.

Mina had a knack for turning every situation into a joke. It annoyed me sometimes because when I wanted to be serious, she kept up with the wisecracks. Still, she was the most dependable person I knew. I could count on her for anything. Sure, she'd pitch a fit at first, but eventually, she'd come around. I had to listen to her complaints, but I was used to that—I just let her talk. She'd vent, and I'd keep asking for what I wanted until she gave in. I was bratty like that.

Hank, though? He was definitely not her better half. I couldn't, for the life of me, understand why she married him. She was too good for him, and their bank accounts never matched. Hank never had a stable job, and he thought selling weed would make him rich. I knew Mina married him because she wanted something completely opposite of herself—and he was exactly that.

Hank stood about 5'11" and weighed 250 pounds. He had brown skin and nice hair. All their kids looked exactly like him, which burned my soul because every time I saw them, all I could see was Hank. Their relationship was strange to me—Mina loved that man's dirty drawers. No matter what he did, she always took his trifling ass back, and it pissed me off. But hey, she loved him. They'd been together for a long time, so who was I to say what worked or didn't? I'd never been married, and I didn't plan on it. I was too busy for all that.

"You're really going to town on that popcorn!" Mina said, raising her eyebrows at me.

I took a drink of soda to wash it down. "Girl, I'm sex-deprived," I laughed. "Besides, they all love my big booty. A little popcorn isn't gonna hurt anything."

I was 5'4" and weighed 185 pounds. If I had to describe myself, I'd say Kanye West was talking about me in *Run This Town*. lot of people said I looked like a mix between Lynn Whitfield and Michelle Williams. I didn't see it, but whatever. I'd always been dramatic, loud, fun, charismatic, loving, outgoing, and independent. I always knew what I wanted out of life, and I did everything without regrets or worries.

"Go ahead and eat your popcorn with those greasy lips," Mina said, continuing to tease me. But I tuned her out and focused on the game, strangely mesmerized by the thumping of the basketball. As the other team played defense, I watched the ball spin in slow motion. Then it stopped for a split second when a certain hand touched it.

Suddenly, my whole world disappeared, and there was nothing left except a tall, dark-brown brother with a nice round ass.

Without taking my eyes off him, I asked Mina, "Who's the nigga in the silver shorts playing against Hank?"

"Oh, I don't know. I think his name is Julian," she said, glancing at the court.

I turned to her with a grin. "Well, tell Hank to introduce me. I gotta hit that."

"You're a nasty bitch, I swear," she laughed.

Reem Denise

After the game ended, Julian came and sat right in front of me. When I handed him my cell phone, he turned around and gave me a look, like he wanted to say, "Bitch, what!"

"Yo, put ya number in my phone so I can call you later," I smiled. "Put me in ya contacts – Ladye Charelle Monroe, no relation to Marilyn."

"Are you serious?" he asked, surprised. "You bold as hell." He started putting his number in my phone, and I chuckled to myself because I knew I had him. To seal the deal, I stood up and walked away slowly, swinging my hips just right to make sure he got a good look at all this ass! I heard the niggas in the gym go, "DAMN!" I walked out knowing I was all that.

"You're a slut," Mina said, trying to burst my bubble.

"Don't hate, Mina. Sometimes you gotta do what you gotta do! And I want that nigga."

Memoirs of an Invisible Woman

The first time Julian and I went on a date, he took me to TGI Friday's. I don't even remember what I ordered because I was too busy staring into those beautiful eyes and admiring his tiny ears. We talked for hours, then hit up a local bar for a few drinks and kept the conversation going. Late into the evening, we ended up at his house, where he had a pool table in his living room.

"Make yourself at home," he said, while I wandered around checking things out. He put the balls in the center of the table, carefully racking them so they stayed nice and tight. Leaning over, he lined up his cue stick and broke the rack. Damn, his ass was fine. I wanted to take a bite of that! But I quickly looked up at him when he turned to see if I was paying attention. I didn't let on that I already knew how to shoot; I just played along.

"So, you use that stick thingy to move the balls?" I asked, pretending. "I don't know how to hold it."

"Come over here," he said, motioning me to the side of the pool table and handing me the cue stick. My body tingled at his touch as he moved one of my legs forward to adjust my stance, then gently pushed my lower back so I'd bend forward. He came up behind me to show me how to hold the stick, and I felt his manhood pressing up against my ass. I couldn't resist—his shaft was huge.

I turned around, grabbed his face with both hands, and kissed him deeply, my tongue hungrily exploring his mouth. We ripped each other's clothes off and stood there for a moment, our eyes drinking in each other's nakedness. Then he picked me up, practically throwing me onto the pool table, and plunged his shaft inside me. That shit was heaven. We've been together ever since.

Memoirs of an Invisible Woman

Twelve Years Later

Julian was everything I could hope for in a man. He was caring, supportive, loving, hardworking, and an excellent father. Whatever I wanted to do, he backed me 100 percent. He was soft-spoken unless he was pissed—then he turned into The Incredible Hulk. Luckily, he smoked mad weed, so he was usually calm.

Now, if you think we lived happily ever after, I've got some swampland in Florida to sell to you. Nah, it wasn't perfect. Yeah, he had a baby on me with his first baby mama while we were supposedly "on a break"—even though it wasn't really a break. His ass was only gone for about a week. When he came back, as usual, he forgot to mention he had slept with Sam. Fast forward nine and a half months, and here comes Juliette, looking exactly like Sam but with Julian's eyes. I loved our girls, but Juliette was a constant reminder that niggas ain't shit and, if you let a dog off the leash for one minute, he'll fuck anything outside the yard.

I wasn't completely innocent either, but I couldn't ever bring myself to tell him about my other life. It would've destroyed us, no questions asked. He would have ghosted me, and knowing him, he would've tried to take the girls with him. That's why I had to do everything possible to keep this shit intact—my whole life depended on it.

When Julian and I first started dating, I had three kids already. My daughter Corey was five at the time, and my boys Seven and Shylo were three and one. They all had the same dad—my high school sweetheart, also named Corey. We had broken up about a year before I met Julian. He gave me my beautiful Jewels, who's eleven, and Reminisce, who's four. Those girls were the apple of their daddy's eye. Julian also had two other kids, Julia and

Juliette, with his triflin' baby mama, Samantha. I loved all the kids, but Samantha? She got on my fuckin' nerves!

Life got crazy sometimes. Besides running my salon, juggling errands, and taking care of the kids, I had to keep my second life a secret—what I did when I went out of town. Most people thought I was going to Houston for hair seminars, but that wasn't the whole truth. Once a month, I flew to Houston, Texas, where I danced at Club Cheetahs. I never let my right hand know what my left hand was doing. My family would never know because I was protecting my kids at all costs. All they would ever know is that I provided for them—whatever it took.

I saved every penny I made. After the kids were taken care of for the month, I gave the rest to Mina. She helped me stash it in three different banks, each with checking and savings accounts.

To keep my secret life under wraps, I always switched up my look. New hairstyle, new me. You never knew who you were getting from day to day. At home, I kept it simple—Plain Jane with a hint of sensuality. But when I hit Houston? Chanelle came out in full force: glamorous makeup, long nails, big lashes, and luxurious hair.

My two worlds were kept completely separate and private. Mina and my best friend Pash were the only ones who knew about what I did in Houston. They never told a soul—not even Hank. I knew I was playing with fire sometimes when I went out of town, but it costs to be a boss! I only let loose in Houston, where I was Chanelle. I loved being her, and she loved me. But when I got home, I was back to being Ladye.

"Good morning," Julian whispered in my ear. "How did you sleep?" I felt him rubbing my ass, which was a clear indication of what was about to go down that morning.

"What time is it?" I asked, rolling over, rubbing my eyes, and stretching deeply.

"It's six. Why? Where do you have to go?"

"Nowhere, baby," I laughed. "I was just asking."

"Oh, okay. I thought you had plans other than giving me some pussy." Just as he finished his sentence, he slid under the covers and started eating my goodies like never before! I tried to squirm away, but he grabbed my legs and locked them with his arms—there was no escape.

"Oh my God, Julian!" I whispered loudly. "Where are the kids? I'm going to scream!" I fought to keep myself in check, but this felt so good. Julian tried to talk to me while he worked his magic down there.

"They're still asleep, and if you have to scream, just use the pillow to cover your mouth," he said in a muffled voice. He opened my legs wider and began to lick my clit like a thirsty man in the desert, pressing two fingers down on my lips. I could feel my clit vibrating, so I grabbed a pillow and put it over my face.

Just as I was about to cum, he stopped licking and pulled his rod out to join the party. I sat up, grabbed his cock, and sucked the hell out of it. I could hear him breathing heavily, trying to compose himself, so I hummed around his throbbing shaft and sucked even harder. I could feel him growing in my mouth, his veins bulging against my lips. I knew he was about to cum, so I pulled him out, flipped him onto the bed, and rode his swollen staff like the Lone Ranger on his horse.

Julian grabbed my ass and pumped into me like we hadn't fucked just a few hours ago. It felt so good that I lost myself in the moment, riding him until I couldn't feel my legs anymore. Just as I was about to cum, he flipped me over, got on top, pushed my legs back to my neck, and fucked me hard. It felt good and bad at the same time, like electric pulses fighting to escape my body. I was about to scream, so he grabbed the pillow.

As I screamed into it, he pounded me even harder. "Julian, please stop!" I begged.

"Nope," he laughed. "Not until you say these are my goodies."

"Julian, you know they're yours!" I screamed.

"Say it then, bitch!" he teased, sweat dripping down his face.

"Julian, this is yours, now and forever. Please stop!" Finally, he came inside me and collapsed, laying on top of me with a devious grin. "Baby number eight just got put in that vagina," he smirked.

"Stop playing with me," I laughed. "We are not having any more kids over here."

Julian hopped out of bed. "I'm about to take a shower, then I'll wake the kids up."

"What do you need me to do?" I asked, stretching lazily.

"You just lay there and remember who your daddy is!" He smiled, closing the bathroom door, then opened it again. "I be fucking the shit out of you, Ladye."

Reem Denise

As he closed the door once more, all I could do was laugh. Honestly, he really did fuck the shit out of me every single time. It just kept getting better and better; each time, I fell in love with him all over again.

Chapter Two

The piercing shrills of my alarm clock ripped me from a deep, heavenly sleep. I opened one eye and slammed my hand on the off button.

"Damn, it's seven already," I groaned. I heard the clomping and pitter-patter of footsteps overhead; the kids were starting to wake up.

"Mommy," a tiny voice whispered.

I sat up, swung my legs over the side of the bed, and yawned. "Yes, Remmie?"

"Daddy won't let me pee-pee," she whined through the door. "I really have to go."

Reem Denise

"Remmie, use the bathroom upstairs. Why is that so hard, little girl? You passed that bathroom to come down the stairs to use this one."

"Mommy, Corey is in that bathroom, and she won't let me pee!" Remmie cried.

I got up and opened the door to see the prettiest little girl staring at me. She was an exact replica of her dad. All I could do was smile as I watched her dance around, trying to hold her legs together. The Dance of the Pee-Pee was a famous ballet in our house. I figured I'd better take action before it was too late.

Remmie, whose real name is Reminisce, was the youngest of the clan. She had brown skin like her dad and long sandy-brown hair that touched the middle of her back. With a small frame like mine, people often asked if she was a mix of Black and Arabian. She wasn't, though; she was just a perfect little girl who was spoiled out of this world.

I walked across the bedroom and knocked on the bathroom door. "Julian, Remmie has to go. Can you stay in the shower until she finishes, please?"

"Little girl, why do you always have to use our bathroom?" he shouted from behind the shower curtain.

"Daddy, your kids keep kicking me out of the other bathroom because they say I take too long to pee. But Daddy, I really don't! I just have to go when I wake up because you told me not to pee in the bed. So, I have to go really bad in the morning!" Remmie exclaimed as she climbed onto the toilet. "Dad, can I go to work with you today? Grandma said I can't come over to her house anymore because I talk too much, and she can't get any work done when I'm over there. So, she told me not to come back today."

"Remmie, your grandmother did not say that," Julian laughed. He knew his mom would never do such a thing.

"Daddy, I promise! Grandma always kicks me out of her house. Poppi told her to stop because he only loves me. He gave me four dollars! Poppi knows I love dollars, Daddy, so he always gives them to me."

"Remmie, are you done using the bathroom?" I asked while checking my face in the mirror.

"Mom, I'm talking to my Daddy because I need to work with him today."

"Girl, stop that whining before I pop you," I said, frowning at her. "You can go to the salon with me. Daddy has a long day and can't take you. Today is too busy."

"Dad, is that true?" she asked.

"Yes, it's true, baby. Daddy has a busy day," he replied.

Remmie looked sadly down at the floor. "Never mind, Mommy. I'll go to my other Grandma's because you take too long, and you're going to try to do my hair. I don't want my hair combed hard today!"

She hopped off the toilet and went to the sink to wash her hands.

"It's a good thing you're cute," I said, sighing. "You are something else, Reminisce."

And she knew it, too. She had me pick her up so she could admire herself in the mirror, and then she nodded her head, indicating she was done.

"Daddy, you can get out of the shower because I'm done. I need cereal, so hurry up and get dressed." Remmie sashayed out of the bathroom, her head held high like the princess she was.

Julian stepped out of the shower, and I slowly handed him a towel to dry off, making sure to sneak an eyeful of that muscular body. His round, smooth ass was tight! He wrapped the towel around his lower half, much to my dismay, and came to stand behind me. When we locked eyes in the mirror, time stood still.

"Ladye, you are so beautiful. I couldn't imagine life without you," he said, kissing my neck.

"As long as you continue to be good to me, you'll never have to," I replied as his lips found mine. I opened the door to leave the bathroom.

"I love you, Ladye!" The way he looked at me sent a thousand shockwaves through my body.

"I love you more, Julian," I winked as I walked back into the bedroom.

I put on my robe and headed to the kitchen to get breakfast started before the kids left for school. I could lie and say I made a gourmet breakfast of eggs, bacon, fruit, and waffles, but the reality was I simply got out the bowls, milk, and cereal. On Wednesdays, it was help-yourself breakfast day because I had to head into the salon. There was no way I was cooking.

The boys clamored down the stairs and rushed into the kitchen, plopping down on the stools at the counter where I had everything laid out. Decked out in polyester basketball shorts and red-and-blue Nike shirts, Seven and Shylo were already taller than me, their gangly legs stretching beneath them. They were still growing into their large feet, rocking the latest Jordans. Seven sported a skin fade with wavy hair on top, while Shylo preferred a tapered look with uniform length. All courtesy of the best hairstylist in the state, of course.

"Good morning! I haven't seen you jerks since last night," I teased.

"Morning, Mom," they replied in unison, grabbing their bowls and pouring in cereal and milk.

"What are your activities for today?"

"Mom, it's Wednesday. We have the same thing every Wednesday: track, then karate," Seven answered, rolling his eyes.

"Okay, smartass. Since you have the answer to everything, who's picking you up and taking you from one place to another?" I asked.

"Dad is coming to get us from school, and he's taking us. We asked him last night," Seven said, taking a spoonful of his cereal.

Shylo piped in, "He's gotta take us to get sneakers today anyway."

"Oh, okay. I didn't talk to your dad, but alright. And what about Corey? Where is that girl?"

Just as I spoke her name, this high-yellow, thick chick came prancing down the stairs as if she owned the house and the world revolved around her.

"Mother," she smirked, knowing I hated when she called me that instead of Mom.

"Corey, keep playing with me, and you're going to get smacked. At 7:30 in the morning, that's a great way to start your day. And what the hell do you have on?" I grimaced at her odd sense of style. She was such a tomboy. "Corey, go take off that stupid-ass jersey and make yourself look like a young lady, please."

"Mom, what's wrong with what I have on?" Corey protested, standing proudly in her outfit: ripped-up jeans she'd made herself, leggings underneath, a Michael Jordan jersey over a white T-shirt, and some Jordan sneakers. Her hair was pulled up into a ponytail, twisted into a bun. When I said she looked like a little-ass teenage boy, I meant it. It drove me crazy.

"Corey, why don't you want to dress like a girl and not always look like your father?" I sighed.

"Seven and Shylo dress like this," she argued.

"Yes, but they are junior high boys. You are not."

"Mom, this is comfortable, and I have basketball practice anyway."

"So, the same clothes you wear to school are the same things you practice in?" I asked.

"No, Mom. I change into my practice stuff, but this is what I like to wear to school."

"Corey, you really give me a headache, and I can't wait until you get out of this phase of looking like a nigga." She ignored me and pulled out her cell to answer a text. I loved her, but she knew which buttons to push.

Just then, Jewels came hopping down the stairs, looking exactly like Julian. "Good morning, Mommy," she said, kissing me on the cheek. Here was my "normal" little girl in her bedazzled blue jeans and butterfly-print sweatshirt. Her hair was neatly braided, adorned with orange beads throughout.

"Hi, Jewels Boo! How did you sleep?"

"I slept good, but I had to keep telling Remmie to get out of my bed. She comes to my room every night and sleeps with me. I hate it!" Jewels grabbed a bowl and a box of cereal.

I turned to see Corey taking a cup out of the cabinet. "Hey, are you eating?"

"No, Mother, I just want some tea." I left her to it and turned back to Jewels. It was pretty typical; there were usually two to five conversations happening at once in our clan.

"Well, Jewels, Remmie loves you and always wants to be close. She looks up to you for protection. It's a big sister thing, just like how you used to look up to Corey until you were old enough to be in your room by yourself."

I bent down to put my forehead against hers, and we both smiled like we had a secret no one else knew about.

"What time is it?" I asked, glancing up.

"It's 7:40," Corey replied.

"Let's go! The bus will be here in a few minutes, and y'all still have to clean up!" Everyone scrambled to finish the last of their breakfast. Within a minute, they washed their dishes, grabbed their coats and backpacks, and rushed out the door. It was always crazy, but I wouldn't trade the chaos for anything in the world.

"I love y'all! See everybody later!" I took my cup of coffee to the opened door—no one ever remembers to close it—as they skipped and ran to the bus stop. It was a sunny but chilly fall morning. Standing on the porch, the hot cup warming my hands, I watched them interact with their friends. I adored them. I would truly be lost without them in my life. At that moment, the people in Houston felt a million miles away, almost as if the club didn't exist. But after the school bus left, I stared down the road, wondering how the weekend would go. My heart skipped a beat at the thought of someone, and I quickly shook it off before walking back inside.

Julian and Remmie had come down to the kitchen. "Are you taking her with you?" I asked. "I thought she was going with me."

"Actually, I'm taking her to your mom's house because that's where she wants to go," Julian said. "She called while we were in the kitchen, so I told your mom I would drop her off on my way to work."

Julian helped Remmie into her coat. She looked adorable in her striped leggings and pink flowered shirt. Her hair was a mess, but I figured Grandma would take care of that.

"Is her bag packed? I thought I had to put some stuff in it," I said, peeking inside. Of course, as usual, it was already ready because I had done it the night before. I handed Julian the bag and picked my daughter up for our daily talk.

"Reminisce, I need you to be on your best behavior because Grandma will whoop your ass. She doesn't play, and I don't want you to get a whoopin' because that would make me sad." I smiled as I kissed her little lips.

"I'm going to be good, Mommy, because Grandma said she got a surprise for me," Remmie beamed.

"Remmie, it's not 'got.' Please don't say 'got' anymore; it works my nerves."

"Okay, Mommy, Grandma has a surprise for me," she said, kissing me back.

"Have a good day, little girl. I love you to the moon and back!" I put her down, and she ran to the door.

"What time are you getting off work?" I asked Julian as he started putting on his coat. He looked good in his tight-fitting jeans, white t-shirt, and Carhartt work boots.

"Probably around five, and I'll pick Remmie up because I have to drive that way to drop something off to my brother. Shouldn't take me too long."

"I have a short day at the salon. I'm just doing inventory and some paperwork. I might do Pascha's hair, but I'm not sure yet."

"Pascha?" Julian looked surprised. "When did she get into town?"

"Last night, probably," I replied, realizing it was time for me to get dressed and ready for work.

"How long is she staying?"

"I'm not sure. Why do you ask?" I glanced over at him, confused by his sudden concern over Pascha.

"Because every time your bestie comes to town, you forget about your family, and all you want to do is party." Julian's irritation was evident as he sat on one of the stools, crossed his arms, frowned, and sulked.

"I don't have plans for a few days, Julian. I have to leave Friday morning anyway, so this week, I'll be concentrating on you guys." I tried to kiss him, but he backed away. I didn't appreciate the disrespect and felt my patience wearing thin.

"Are you serious right now, Julian? You're mad about nothing. It's too early for this! Pascha is here on family business."

"Yeah, right," he huffed.

"I'm serious! She needs to take care of her father. And she'll be coming over to see her godchildren if his royal highness doesn't mind," I said sarcastically.

"Ladye, stop playing with me." Julian stood up to pace back and forth in front of the kitchen counter. "She can come see the kids anytime she wants. I know these are her babies, and she loves the hell out of them. I'm just talking about you two together; it never goes well..."

As Julian continued to lecture me about the crazy stuff Pascha and I used to do, I tuned out his voice and, without meaning to, relived bits of forbidden memories. Usually, I refused to indulge in these fantasies, but they were nearly impossible to forget, especially since they had become almost a regular thing. Small visions would come to me when I least expected it: a mischievous smile, the strength of a muscular back, the scent of Kenneth Cole cologne as I kissed someone's cheek, or strong hands massaging my body. More and more, I seemed to immerse myself in the ecstasy that I had no right to experience.

Suddenly, I realized Julian had stopped talking, so I pretended there was lint on my blouse, hoping he wouldn't see the guilt on my face. This was my fiancé, and I owed him my love and loyalty. He could never find out.

"Baby, are you okay?"

"I'm fine, sweetness. I think I must be starting my period or something. Just feeling a little lightheaded."

"You sure?" He seemed to forget his anger about Pascha being in town.

"You always take care of me," I said, leaning against him. He wrapped his arms around me and nuzzled my neck.

"Hey, you'd better get going before Remmie learns to drive your truck," I giggled. "Julian, I love you. Go have a beautiful day at work, and dinner will be ready when you get home."

Reem Denise

He kissed me long and hard, then, without a word, winked and left the house. I leaned in the doorway, thankful he hadn't seen the change in me, and waved as he and Remmie drove away.

Chapter Three

The uplifting voices of Hezekiah Walker and his choir drifted through the surround sound system as I got ready for work. The rich textures and conviction of their harmonies permeated my very soul. His rousing words of brotherhood, hope, and prayer always made me feel like jumping up and praising God myself.

It was a perfect way to start the day. Singing along with Mr. Walker, I straightened our bedroom and cleaned up the kitchen. I liked having an organized, spotless home, and I hated coming back to a mess after a long day.

After hopping into the shower, I dressed in a comfortable yet stylish sweatsuit and matching tennis shoes. I loved being my own boss! Sitting down to make phone calls and check messages, I came across a promising email. A company wanted me to teach a few classes during the week on different braid techniques to cosmetology students. They needed an answer by that evening, so I decided to give them a call first thing. I never passed up an opportunity to teach younger stylists my craft or make extra money if I could squeeze it into my schedule.

"Hello, United School of Cosmetology, this is Lauren speaking. How may I help you?"

"Hi Lauren, my name is Ladye Monroe. I received an email from Cathy Chancellor regarding teaching some classes, and I was wondering if she was available to speak with me?"

"Can you hold for a moment, Ms. Monroe? I'll see if she's in her office."

"Yes, I'll hold."

"Thank you."

Memoirs of an Invisible Woman

She placed me on hold, and I was greeted by the sound of soft elevator music—Kenny G or something similar.

"Good morning, this is Cathy," came a bubbly voice, soft-spoken and warm.

"Hello, Cathy. My name is Ladye, and I received your email about teaching some braiding classes for your students. I wanted to check if the position is still open and if you could tell me a little more about it."

"Oh, Ladye, I'm so glad you called! Your name has come up in several meetings because you're apparently one of the top braiders in the city, and you come highly recommended."

"Oh my gosh, thank you so much for saying that! I had no idea! It's really kind of people to think that about me. I work hard and strive to please everyone I meet."

"Well, the position is on Monday, Tuesday, and Wednesday nights from 3:00 PM to 7:00 PM, and one Saturday a month from 9:00 AM to 2:00 PM. Is that something you can manage?"

"Cathy, anything is possible, but how long is this for?" I asked, trying to gauge the commitment.

"Well, right now, we want to try it for six months and see how it goes, with the possibility of extending it for a year."

"Oh, okay. That sounds exciting," I said, doing my best to suppress my enthusiasm. I wanted to maintain the upper hand. "I'll need to check with my family to see if that's feasible. I want to ensure it's a good fit for everyone involved. Can I ask how much the position pays?"

"Well, Ladye, it's $15.00 an hour, but that's negotiable because we really want you to teach the class. We do have some wiggle room in the budget. Is it possible for you to come in for an interview with the board of directors to discuss this further?"

"Of course, Cathy! Just let me know what day you need me to come in, and I'll be there."

"Can you come next Tuesday, the 18th, at 1:00 PM? Is that convenient for you?"

"Yes, I can do that, Cathy. It's not a problem."

"Okay, Ladye, I look forward to seeing you next week."

"You as well, Cathy. Thank you so much for taking the time to speak with me."

"Oh no, thank you for responding to my email so quickly. Have a good day!"

"You too, Cathy."

I hung up the phone, filled with elation. I couldn't believe I was about to be a teacher. Who would have ever thought?

Just then, my phone rang again. I picked it up, still buzzing from my new opportunity.

"Good morning, bitch!" The squeaky laughter was unmistakable.

"Good morning, Pash," I replied. "What are you doing up this early?"

"Nothing much, just checking in. Are you going to do my hair today or tomorrow?"

"Whenever, Pash! It doesn't matter to me. I have to go to the shop anyway to do some inventory and paperwork, so I guess today works fine."

"What time do you want me to come?" she asked.

"How about noon?"

"I'll be ready! Want me to bring some wine? We have a lot of catching up to do," she snickered.

"Oh God, what are you giggling about? You must be up to something, Pash, and I'm not about to get roped into your shenanigans," I sighed. "I already got the third degree from Julian this morning, all because you're in town."

"What? Why?"

"Because he seems to think that when we're together, it's nothing but trouble."

"That's ridiculous! Just because we get drunk every once in a while… okay, a lot," she admitted. "And maybe we flirt a little… all right, sleep around, but no one needs to know that."

"Remember when we had too many Long Island iced teas and went dancing in the park sprinklers?"

"I never did find my panties," Pash said, cracking up. "Oh, and remember the twins? Michael and Malik?"

"Girl, don't get me hot and bothered this early in the day!" I cried, biting my knuckles.

"I don't know what Julian is worried about. I'm sweet and innocent. Pure as the driven snow."

"You keep telling yourself that," I chuckled. "Girl, we've had some crazy adventures. And he doesn't even know about all of them. But he didn't need to get all defensive before the day even started."

"Does he suspect anything about Houston?"

"Shut your mouth!" I glanced over my shoulder as if someone might be listening. "I don't think so. I think he was just paranoid for no reason this morning."

"Well, you know what happens in Houston stays there. My lips are sealed. He doesn't need to worry. Not today, anyway," she said. "I just miss my best friend, and I want to talk to her and laugh about our shit!"

"That's what friends are for!" I looked at the clock and realized I needed to get my act together. "Okay, girl, I'll see you at noon. I have to get my life in order, and you're slowing me down. Love ya! Later!"

Reem Denise

As I finished up my emails, I thought about Pascha. She'd been my best friend for over 15 years. It was kind of strange how we actually became friends. We used to go to the same church, and she hung out with this woman named Glenda, who everyone considered a troublemaker. Actually, a better word for her was busybody. She knew every church member's business, and it was quite annoying. At first, Pascha and I had nothing to do with each other because I didn't mess with busybodies, nor did I do church people like that. I just went to hear the word and leave; it was better that way. I wasn't interested in gossip. To me, that wasn't the Christian way.

One day, Pash, a few others, and I were at Glenda's house for her nephew's 25th birthday party. It was actually a lot of fun, and I had a chance to get to know Pash and really talk to her. I realized she was actually really cool.

Memoirs of an Invisible Woman

When I saw her in church that next Sunday, I approached her and said, "I need to apologize. I judged you because you're friends with Glenda, and I figured you were a busybody like her. I'm sorry."

She laughed and replied, "Actually, I was feeling the same way about you, but I accept your apology."

We've been best friends ever since.

Pash was 38 years old, standing at about 5 feet tall, with a high yellow complexion. I loved her hazel eyes, which changed with her emotions. She got her long dark brown hair from her ancestors because she was half Indian. I kept telling her she had a nice shape, but for some reason, she thought she needed work done. She had 38D breasts, an okay butt, and that squeaky voice was loud as hell. Sometimes I had to tune her out because her shrill voice drove me crazy. Pash also had two of the most handsome sons, Tyreem and Savion. I loved those boys to pieces.

Suddenly, the phone rang, breaking my train of thought. "Hello, this is Ladye. How may I help you?" I said in my most professional voice, as if I were already at work. "I mean, hello!"

"Well, hey there," Julian laughed. "Ladye, you had a moment, huh?"

"Yeah, I do that sometimes," I said, shaking my head. "Hi, honey! How are you?"

"I'm doing just fine. I was calling to check on you and see what you have planned for the day because I forgot your truck needs to go to the shop for servicing. They just called to remind me. I was going to come home and switch vehicles with you so I can take your car."

"Well, I'm actually on my way to the shop in about ten minutes, but you can meet me there," I said.

"That'll work. I'll meet you there around noon."
"Perfect, babe. See you then." I hung up the phone, grabbed my laptop and coat, turned off the lights, and headed out the door.

Chapter Four

I pulled up to the shop, already aggravated before I even turned off the engine. The salon windows were filthy, which meant the cleaning crew hadn't come that Sunday as scheduled. Of course, the payment had already been deducted from my account.

Muttering a few choice words under my breath, I got out of my car, slammed the door, and marched into my shop. When I flicked the lights on, the salon looked exactly as I had left it on Saturday, complete with overflowing wastebaskets. I surveyed my four-station salon, simple yet cozy, with a tall front counter and a little waiting area furnished with comfortable chairs and an abundance of beauty magazines. Plenty of natural light streamed through the front windows, complemented by the fluorescents. The building itself wasn't that old, so the light burgundy and pink walls still appeared fresh. I had decorated with lots of plants and photos of stunning hairstyles. I loved my little place—even when it was dirty.

Just as I was about to call the cleaning company, Pash strutted in.

"Hey, chick!" She grabbed me in a big hug.

"Hey, Pash! You look great! You're slimming down like crazy," I said, pushing her back to get a good look at her.

"Yeah, we'll talk about that too," she smirked.

"Have a seat; I'll get you started right after I make this damn phone call."

I tapped my fingernails on the front counter as I waited for someone to answer. Once I was on hold again, I switched to speaker.

"EZ Cleaning Company, this is Rosalind. How may I help you?"

"Hi, Rosalind. This is Ladye Monroe over at the Beauty is Beautiful Hair Salon. I was wondering why my shop hasn't been cleaned. You charged me for it, and I'm pretty pissed that it's still dirty."

"Ms. Monroe, I apologize for that. We sent you an email on Sunday because our cleaning truck broke down. However, we will be there today by three to clean the entire shop. I wasn't aware that the payment had already been deducted from your account. I will also add a seventy-five-dollar credit to your account for the next time we come out. Again, I apologize for the inconvenience, and we'll be there shortly."

"Thank you so much, Rosalind. I didn't finish reading my emails this morning, so I appreciate you messaging me. I'll be on the lookout for you guys. Thank you and have a good day!"

"You do the same, Ms. Monroe. We really appreciate your business." I hung up the phone and breathed a sigh of relief.

"That was pleasant," Pash said. "You were ready to go off, and she was so sweet you couldn't even do it if you tried. She melted you like butter."

"I know, right? She was so damn nice I almost said never mind, I'll clean it myself. Her customer service skills are on point; they'd better never lose her."

Pash was sitting in a styling chair, so I twirled it around to check out her hair. "Hey, gorgeous, what do you want me to do with your hair? And don't even think about cutting it! That's not happening."

"Girl, shut up, I already know. I think I want a spiral roller set, and can I get some highlights if possible?"

"Of course you can." I went to grab a cape to get Pash started just as Julian walked in.

"Hey, Julian," Pash called out.

"What's up, Pascha? How have you been?" He walked over and kissed her on the cheek. "You're looking good, girl!"

"Thank you very much," she beamed. "I'm trying to work out and get my body like Ladye's."

"Oh, okay, cool." He turned to me. "Babe, can I have the key? I'm already running behind."

He stood there, holding his hand out, while I gave him a playful stare. "Of course you can, but do I get a kiss too?"

"I'm sorry, baby, it just slipped my mind that quick," he said, leaning in to kiss me. I loved how great his breath always smelled.

"Are you cooking tonight, L?" he asked.

"Yes, honey, I am cooking. Is there anything specific you want?"

"The boys said they wanted pepper steak and rice, so that works for me."

"No problem, I got y'all covered."

"Okay, ladies, see y'all later," he said, grabbing the keys from me. "I gotta go run these errands. I love you, Ladye."

"I love you more, babe." Julian walked out of the salon and hopped into my truck.

"Aww, you guys are perfect," Pash said.

"Bitch, please, everything that glitters is not gold," I said as I shook out the cape before draping it around her neck. "Julian's got his shit with him, and so do I. We just try to keep it together for the girls."

"Do you think he cheats?" Pash asked, settling back into the chair.

"I don't put anything past anyone, not even Julian. I've been through a lot of dumb shit with him; I just don't let it be known. We don't air our business, but trust me, we go through the same struggles as all couples. We just keep it together for our family. He's a man's man. His parents raised him to always provide for his family and let nothing come to his doorstep."

"Sounds like you have a good hold on things," she said.

"I'd like to think so," I replied. "Come on, I'll have you shampooed and out of here before the cleaning crew arrives."

We went back to the shampoo room so I could get Pash started with her highlights. "Ladye, you and Julian will be fine," she assured me.

"I know we will, but we're not perfect. Now, change the subject. How are you losing all this weight? I love it, but don't get any smaller or you gon' look like a crackhead!" We both burst out laughing.

"I started working out at first, but the weight wasn't coming off fast enough for me, so I had the Lap-Band done about two months ago, and I love the results. I still work out, but I wanted the weight off quicker because I felt fat and ugly."

"Pash, you have never been ugly! Fat, yes; ugly, no!"

She good-naturedly slapped me. "Fuck you, bitch, you just jealous."

"Let me look at these highlights." I removed one of the foils to see what color her hair had changed to. "Pash, it's a pretty blonde. You want to be lighter than this?" I handed her a mirror.

"Oh no, Ladye, this is perfect."

"Okay, let me rinse it out then." I rinsed the bleach out of her hair and began to shampoo it.

"OH MY GOD, nobody shampoos hair like you!" she moaned, sounding like the star of a low-budget porn show.

"Thanks, girl, but don't be getting off on me shampooing your hair! That shit is disgusting, so stop making those stupid noises, you skank."

"That's Ms. Skank to you, heiffa."

After I sat Pash under the dryer with her conditioner, I grabbed my laptop to start looking over books. It wasn't a bad week at the salon. Everyone seemed to have a lot of money, which was always good because I loved this business. I wanted to keep profiting and taking care of my family, friends, and employees. Everyone got to eat at this salon.

"Ladye, my dryer went off!" Pash yelled across the room.

"Okay, you know what to do! Go to the shampoo room! I'll be there in a second!" I had no clue why I was yelling. Pash was loud, and it seemed contagious because everyone around her always talked louder than they normally would.

I walked back to the shampoo room to rinse out her conditioner. "How come no matter how close we are, your ass is always yelling?"

"Honestly, I think it's from having a half-deaf mother," Pash replied. "I always had to yell for her to hear me, so I just assume everyone is deaf, I guess."

"You know the weird part about that, Pash?" I asked. "It actually makes sense. Now I understand why you're so loud. As annoying as it is, I get it."

"Why, thank you for your kindness," she said sarcastically. "Should I be insulted that you find me annoying?"

"You are not annoying. Your loud voice is annoying."

"That's the same thing."

"Oh, just shut up and go to the styling chair." We both smirked at each other while I rolled her hair. I was glad she was there, but sometimes I needed a mental break from my best friend. Or maybe I just needed a moment to myself. Anyway, her hair took forever because she had so much of it, but the end result was always fabulous.

After I finished, I felt more relaxed, and Pash was quietly, if you can believe it, humming to herself. I sat her under the dryer and went back to my laptop to pay some bills and make sure the lights stayed on. Just as I was catching up on emails, there was a knock at the door.

"You guys don't have the key?" I asked as I let the cleaning crew in.

"Yes, ma'am, but we noticed the car outside, so we figured someone was here and didn't want to startle anyone. We usually come on Sundays when no one's around at all," one of the gentlemen said.

"That makes sense. Well, I'll actually be done in about a half hour if you want to start in the break room and work your way up to the front. Then I'll be out of your way," I smiled.

"That's not a problem, ma'am," he replied.

"Sir, what is your name?" I asked, giving him the evil eye.

"Mario, why?"

"Because, Mario, I am 34 years old, and it bothers me when a man who looks close to my age calls me ma'am," I said with just a little attitude.

"My fault. I apologize. What is your name, if I may ask?"

"Yes, you may, and my name is Ladye. I'm fine with being called Ladye."

"Well, Ladye it is." He smiled and tipped his baseball cap in a distinguished manner.

It was hard to stay mad at that. "Thank you, Mario."

As they headed toward the break room, I checked on Pash under the dryer. "Who was that?" she asked.

"Just the cleaning guys."

"Well, he was sexy," she said, licking her lips.

"Pash, shut the hell up. You think every man is hot." We both laughed. He was pretty fine, but I wasn't going to tell her that because her weird ass would start trying to hook people up. She swore she was the Love Doctor to all the side chicks.

Reem Denise

She thought she was wise and powerful, but all Pash knew was how to give love advice to chicks already sleeping with somebody else's man. The thing was these bitches really listened to her and actually paid her for that stupid-ass advice. What she never told them was what would happen if they got caught. Besides being labeled a homewrecker, the side chick got pummeled by the main bitch nine times out of ten.

These girls had no common sense and never really considered the consequences. If they knew, they might not have taken those odds.

I thought the whole situation was really dumb, and I couldn't believe these chicks could possibly take her seriously. But honestly, they hung on to her every word. They called her the Love Guru of Houston, and that drove me mad when I went to visit her.

"Are you coming to H-Town this weekend?" she asked.

"Of course. I have to work, don't I?"

"Actually, you don't have to work; you choose to work, Ladye," she said tartly.

"Oh, so you're going to support my kids through private school and pay for my retirement? Yes, I do have to work if I want those things."

I looked her in the eyes, waiting for her to respond with something smart-alecky because I was ready for her. We were about to have a battle of the mouths, and I was not in the mood for any lectures from this bitch.

"I'm just sayin'," Pash sneered. "Sure, you're making money, but look at what else you're doing. Is it worth the risk?"

"Once again, little girl, I'm trying to make money to support my family!" I said through clenched teeth. "Who the fuck do you think you are, getting in my business and trying to lecture me about how I live my life? I know what I'm doing, 'Miss Pure as the Driven Snow,' and my family is more important to me than anything!"

"Then why doesn't Julian know about your other job? You know he wouldn't approve of it, and you're having an awful lot of fun doing it." She trailed off softly when she saw the veins bulging out of my forehead. She knew better than to push me. When I was in Ohio, I was

Ladye, and Houston was a million miles away. It was worlds away. And that's the way I liked it. That's why I didn't want to talk about it.

I was so angry I was afraid I'd hit her, so I started ripping the rollers out of her hair quickly to get her out of my shop.

Suddenly, she grabbed my arm, forcing me to look at her. "I'm sorry, Ladye," she said softly, tears in her eyes. "I really overstepped my boundaries, didn't I?"

"And then some." I was still pissed, but I pulled the rollers out a little slower and gentler.

"I don't even know what to say, Pash," I said, shaking my head. "You know me better than that. I don't like to be disrespected. If it were anybody else, you'd be down on the floor, crying because you got the shit slapped out of you."

"I totally believe it. I don't know why I kept pressing it, except that I'm worried about you. About these two lives you're living and how easily it can be to fuck up . . ."

She stopped talking when I put my hand up, palm facing outward. "Stop right there," I said. "You need to back the fuck up. I need you to promise not to bring it up again. It's my life, and I'll live it the way I choose. I want your word."

Pash sighed and ran her fingers through her curls.

"I mean it, Pash. You're my best friend, but that doesn't give you the right to judge me or assume that you know everything. I'm glad it's come to this because it feels like you've been in my business way too much lately, and it's like you're always on the verge of saying something. When I'm here, I'm Ladye—the woman engaged to Julian, raising five kids, and running a salon. End of story."

"Okay, girl. You know I love and respect you more than anyone else in the world. You're right; I'm too nosy for my own good," she said, standing up. "Can I have a hug? Do you forgive me?"

I hesitated, pretending to think about it. But I'll always love Pascha. "Come here," I sighed. "I don't know what I'm gonna do with you."

Reem Denise

After we squeezed the stuffing out of each other, I made her sit back down so I could check out those beautiful curls.

"Not to push my luck but are we going out for drinks tonight?" she asked.

"No, I'm at the house tonight. I stayed in during the week so that when I leave on Friday morning, I don't have to hear Julian's mouth about not spending any family time. But you're more than welcome to come over for some wine and to visit your godchildren. I'm sure the kids would love to see you, plus I'm cooking dinner. I know how your greedy ass loves to eat," I snickered.

"You know what? You are absolutely right; I do love to eat, and I would love to see my babies. Plus, I've got to give them the presents I bought. Last time I came, I didn't bring them anything, and Remmie cussed me out," she giggled. "That little girl is something else. I can't with her."

"Girl, Remmie is truly in a league of her own," I agreed. "She keeps me on my toes. I know, in about four years, I'm going to have to kill her because she swears she knows everything. She's so confrontational! She gets that from Julian, you know."

"Oh yeah, blame Remmie on Julian because she acts exactly like you to a tee," Pash roared. "The only thing she has of Julian is her face and hair; everything else is all you."

I spun the chair around so she could see her hair, and she screamed with glee. "Oh my god, Ladye, it is gorgeous! As usual. I love this color! You know you keep me poppin'. I love my hairdresser, sister, and best friend. All those Houston bitches are gonna be so jealous when they see this half-breed step on the scene," she yelled, her voice getting louder, if that's even possible. "But they're always jealous anyway, so it doesn't matter."

"Pash, get out of my chair. You're making my head hurt again," I joked. I took the cape from around her neck, and she stood up, stretching her legs and letting out a loud yawn.

"You wanna walk out together?"

"No, you go ahead. I'm about to leave; I just want to make sure these guys are cool and have everything they need. I'm going straight home after that to start cooking, so you can come over anytime if you just want to hang out."

"I'll come over after I see my mom and dad because I'll be in the doghouse if they find out I was in town and didn't stop by to see them. You know my mom! She is so dramatic and swears her kids don't love her!"

"Yeah, you'd better go see them."

"Okay, I'm leaving. One more hug!" She lunged at me with her arms straight out like Frankenstein or something. I gave her a quick hug, like she was scaring me, then pushed her away.

"Now get out!" I laughed.

"Well, bye, bitch, I love you too," she smirked.

"I love you more!"

The cleaning crew were all set and promised to text pictures showing that the place was locked up. I left the shop and headed home to start dinner before my own crazy crew invaded the house.

Chapter Five

I was lost in thought as I finished making the pepper steak for dinner. Stirring the beef strips, bamboo shoots, onions, bean sprouts, and slices of bell peppers, I greedily inhaled the aroma of ginger and soy sauce. As I tasted a small spoonful, I glanced at the clock—it was 5:30 p.m.

"Where the hell is my family?" I muttered.

No sooner had I spoken those words than I heard little footsteps running through the house toward the kitchen.

"Hi, Mommy!" Remmie screamed.

"Well, hi, Remmie! Why are you so loud? I can hear, you know."

She grabbed my legs and squeezed them with an aggressive sort of love. "I'm hungry, Mommy, and Grandma only fed me cake!" she said, looking up at me with her innocent face.

"Remmie, I'm sure Grandma fed you more than cake. Grandma always has food because she's my mom, and we all love to eat." I gave her *the look* that makes all children uncomfortable—one brow arched with laser-ready eyes that can penetrate your very soul. "So, what did you eat today, Reminisce Simone?"

She tried to stand her ground for a minute, but I've been around the block a time or two. "Oh, that's right. I forgot, Mommy. I ate cereal in the morning with coffee and toast. For lunch, I had steak with mashed potatoes and corn. And then Grandma gave me cake. Me and Poppi ate it with some milk, and it was so good!" She released my legs as she spoke, thinking I might pop her for lying.

"Yeah, I thought so, little girl." I grabbed her face and kissed her. "You are such a pretty girl. Now, where is Jewels?"

"She went straight upstairs because she and Daddy were arguing in the car about a grade she got." Remmie was more than happy to report on someone else's misfortunes, especially since the focus was now off of her. "Jewels was mad because Daddy took her phone, and she said Daddy is never fair. Mommy, Daddy was so mad he told her to go to her room as soon as we got home, and that's why she went upstairs without saying hi to you!" Remmie skipped around the kitchen table to sit in her favorite chair.

"Thank you, Remmie. You're just a regular walking Eyewitness News. Where is your dad?" I asked.

"He went to your bedroom, Mommy," she said, playing with the mail on the table, like she was about to pay a bill or something.

I went upstairs to find Julian lying in bed with his phone, looking like he was texting somebody.

"Who are you on the phone with?" I asked. He jumped up as if I startled him.

"Why the fuck are you acting like you're sneaking around on the phone?" I yelled. "Who you texting, the bitch you're sleeping with?" I shook my head in pure disgust.

"Ladye, shut the fuck up! Ain't nobody texting no fucking bitch. Stop being so fucking paranoid," he said as he put the phone on the home screen.

"Asshole, I'm far from paranoid. Shit, I don't give a fuck as long as it doesn't come across my door, you fucking prick," I replied, gearing up for the real argument. "Now, what the fuck happened with Jewels that made you think you could take her phone—the one that I pay for?" I crossed my arms and tapped my foot, waiting for a response.

"Ladye, first of all, watch your fuckin' mouth," he growled as he sat on the edge of the bed, clenching his fists. "I don't give a fuck who paid for the phone. If I tell my fuckin' daughter she can't have the fuckin' phone, then she can't have it! Ain't no fuckin' way you gon' tell me how to discipline my daughter in my fuckin' house! If you don't like my fuckin' rules, you can fuckin' move out! But at the end of the day, I'm going to raise my daughter to have her shit together. Bottom line! Now get your ass the fuck out of my face before this shit goes entirely to the fuckin' left!"

I didn't doubt things could turn ugly, but I wasn't about to back down. "Oh shit, I guess you finally got some balls. You want to be a disciplinarian to our kids, but you don't have shit to say to your bitch over there with your other two bastards! Get the fuck out of here! Give me the fuckin' phone and find some other type of punishment, because she's not gon' be out there without a fuckin' phone. If something happens to my baby, then I gotta kill your stupid ass because she couldn't call us because her dumbass father took her phone! Don't play with me about these fuckin' kids! I would've thought you knew by now that I will fight you or anyone else when it comes to them!"

The more I yelled, the more he seemed to shrink in size and confidence. I stuck my hand out, and he reluctantly handed me the phone. "Ladye, this is far from over. I'm sick of you not letting me be a father to my kids."

I didn't think of myself as a vicious woman, but it took all my inner strength not to tear his head off. "Julian, who is this conversation for? Me or Samantha? I don't stop you from doing shit, but do things that make sense. That was Jewels's first low grade ever! It's stupid to take her phone for that reason."

Suddenly, the front door alarm buzzed, and I could hear one of the kids talking to someone. "Mom!" Shylo yelled from downstairs. I opened the bedroom door and yelled back, "What boy? Stop yelling in MY DAMN HOUSE!" I emphasized *the house* to make sure Julian heard me loud and clear. I didn't know who the fuck he thought he was talking to, but I rained on his parade real quick.

"Fuckin' asshole, who does he think he's talking to?" I mumbled, shutting the bedroom door behind me.

"What, Mom?" Shylo asked as he came down the hallway.

"Nothing, Shylo. What can I help you with, son?"

"My dad needs to talk to you for a second; he's in the hallway," he replied.

As I walked down the stairs, I saw Corey, my ex, standing in the doorway. "Hey, Core, what's up?"

"Nothing much, I just wanted to talk to you about something," he said, beads of sweat glistening on his forehead as he wiped his palms on his pants.

"Really, Corey? What's on your mind?"

"Well… um… I think the boys should live with me for a few months." He stepped back, as if he expected me to slap him.

"Why would they need to live with you? Where is this coming from? Am I missing something?" I asked.

"No, you're not. I just think the boys are at an age where they need to live with me for a while."

I tried to breathe deeply to release the pain in my heart. "Corey, let me think about it. I wasn't expecting this at all. I'm not saying no; just let me talk to them," I said.

"Okay, Ladye, let me know soon. I really want the boys. But I'm sure Corey doesn't want to live with me because she probably wants her privacy, and living with her dad isn't going to cut it. But if she wants to, I'd love to have her."

He pushed it too far. I just couldn't take it anymore. "Corey, get the hell out of my house!" I screamed, grabbing a vase. He opened the front door, his eyes wide in fear. "You're definitely not taking Corey. That is my baby, so you can forget it!"

He ran out and slammed the door, barely escaping the vase I aimed at his head. I stared at the pieces on the floor, feeling completely drained after my earlier fights with Pash and Julian. How could Corey break my heart so quickly? Who would have thought he was coming to tell me he wanted my boys? And to even suggest I let him take my daughter was too much.

The front door creaked open about half an inch. "Ladye? It's me, Pash! I saw Corey running. Is it safe?"

"Yeah, come on in," I sighed, grabbing the broom and dustpan from the hall closet.

"What did I miss? I don't think I've ever seen Corey move that fast," she asked.

"Girl, nothing, just Corey deciding he wants to be daddy of the year. We'll talk later; I was just about to call the kids down for dinner."

As we walked to the kitchen, I yelled, "Kids, come and eat before the food gets cold!" Suddenly, it sounded like a stampede as a bunch of water buffalo came charging down the stairs. We stepped aside to avoid being trampled as the herd raced by. When we caught up to them in the kitchen, they realized their godmother was there.

"Auntie Pash, where did you come from?" Corey asked.

"I came from the front door. Now give me a hug while you ask silly questions," Pash laughed. All the kids rushed over to hug her, except for Jewels, who was still sulking about her phone.

"Nish, what's wrong, baby?" Pash asked.

"Nothing, Godmommy. My dad just took my phone."

Remmie had to chime in. "Yeah, she got in trouble today."

"Shut up, you ugly snitch! All you do is talk; that's why we don't like you now!" Jewels yelled.

"Watch your mouth, Jewels, before I pop you," I warned. "I understand you're mad, but don't come for my baby. Here is your stupid phone."

Jewels instantly brightened. "Thank you, Mom! How did you get it? Dad said I couldn't have it for two weeks."

"Never mind that, but you better get it together in school and study before I beat your ass!"

"Mom, Dad went nuts for no reason, though. All I did was get an 80 on a spelling test because I missed two words, and he went crazy on me." Her eyes filled with tears.

"Jewels, you better not start crying with your sensitive self," I said, putting my arm around her. "It's okay. I handled your father. Next time, just try to get a

100." Julian was really in trouble; taking my baby's phone over a stupid 80 on a spelling test was just ridiculous. He was such an overreactor; I hated when he pulled that kind of dumb shit.

"Everybody sit down and eat. Remmie, can you ask your dad if he wants a plate for me, please?" Remmie dashed to the bedroom, and I knew she'd be quick.

"Mommy, he said no. He's tired and going to sleep."

"Oh, okay. Well, sit down and eat your food." Everyone seemed to enjoy their dinner. I served pepper steak with rice and gravy, broccoli, and cornbread. They ate like I didn't cook every other night.

"So, boys, what's this about y'all wanting to live with your dad?" I asked. "You don't want to live with me anymore?" I didn't look at them, trying to hold back the tears.

"Of course we do, Mom. It's just that we're becoming young men, and we thought maybe living with Dad would be easier," Seven said.

"Easier for who? I can't imagine my house without my boys; I would miss y'all like crazy! I love all of you to death, and my life without y'all would be nothing."

The table fell silent as the boys exchanged nervous glances.

"I put everything into raising you, but whatever you decide, I support you," I said, taking a deep breath and putting on my best smile. "So, if you guys want to try living with him for a month, we can give it a shot."

Everyone let out a big sigh. "Mom, for real?" Shylo asked, grinning from ear to ear.

"Yes, for real. I guess you guys need to be with your dad more anyway. Corey, are you going too?"

She looked at me like I'd grown antlers. "Umm, no! Why would I want to live with Corey? Bad enough I have to share his name."

"Really, Corey? I love your name; that's why I named you that," I laughed.

"I love my name, too. I just wish I wasn't named after my father," she said, rolling her eyes.

"Oh, I see what you're saying, but it is a cute name," I said.

"I guess, Mom." She smacked her lips in mild annoyance.

After dinner, we lingered at the kitchen table, chatting. Pash opened her purse and handed each kid a card. "Thank you, Auntie!" Corey exclaimed, planting a kiss on her cheek.

The kids squealed with excitement; they knew Pash spoiled them rotten. "Okay, you guys have visited with your aunt enough. Give kisses and go get ready for bed," I said. "We have school tomorrow, and I don't want any mess in the morning. Make sure y'all brush your teeth and knock on the door to tell Julian goodnight. I'll be up in a few to check on you. I love y'all; sleep tight!"

"Okay, Mom, goodnight!" They raced upstairs, and I could hear them knocking on my bedroom door.

"I cannot believe how well you have them on a schedule! They do it like it's nothing," Pash said, admiration shining in her eyes. "I have my nephews and nieces over sometimes, and I'm ready to kill them by the end of the night!"

"Want a glass of wine?" I offered. "We can head to the living room and chit-chat for a bit, but it won't be long. I've got a long day tomorrow."

Once we settled in the living room, Pash reached over and touched my hand. "Are you doing okay? You look exhausted."

"Normally, I'd take that as an insult, but I feel like I look," I replied with a weary smile. "Girl, it's been a long day."

"Sorry about our fight earlier."

"That was just the beginning. I was okay after that, but then I had a huge fight with Julian, and after that, Corey came asking for my boys." I struggled to hold back the tears; I wasn't ready to cry. I just wanted to enjoy a moment with my best friend.

Pash knew exactly how to distract me. She brought up some friends she'd been wondering about, and we reminisced about old times like we always did, talking about people we hadn't seen in years.

"When are you going back to Houston?" I asked.

"Friday, first flight out, I think. The 5:45 AM flight," she said.

"Oh, me too! What airline are you flying?"

"The same one we always fly, Ladye. Southwest," she laughed. "I booked us together on purpose."

"Oh, hell no! We're on the same flight? This is going to be crazy! Well, cool, I can ride to the airport with you. That way, Julian doesn't have to get up and drop me off. He'd be pissed if I woke him up that early."

"Yeah, I'm sure. That works for me. How long are you staying? For the weekend again?"

"Yep, I'll be right back on the first flight out Sunday morning. You know I go to do my job and then I bounce," I laughed. She made no mention of our earlier argument; she knew better.

"Yeah, I know. Well, I need to get ready to go because I have some errands to run early in the morning with my mom. You know she gets up at the crack of dawn and starts giving out demands as soon as she brushes her teeth."

We both cracked up. "Okay, girl. Stop by the shop tomorrow when we're open if you can. I'm sure the crew would love to see your nutty ass!"

"Will do, bestie. Love ya!"

"Love ya more!"

After I watched her drive away, I sank into one of the porch rockers, the weight of the day finally lifting. I loved my family and friends, but I was so glad this day was over. Closing my eyes, I practiced some deep breathing, just like I learned in yoga class. The combination of that and the wine with Pash made me feel a lot more relaxed than I had all day.

I felt ready to face Julian. The anger had ebbed away, and I still loved that sexy man. A smile crept onto my face as I thought, "Hmm, what can we do that would make both of us feel better?"

Chapter Six

I fantasized about the things I would do to the sexy man in my bedroom, but I decided to make him suffer just a little longer. First, I wanted to enjoy the quietness of the house and straighten up a bit.

I went upstairs to check on the kids; it was funny how they looked like perfect angels when they were sleeping. Even though this family was dramatic and chaotic at times, I could count on them to have their heads on their pillows like clockwork. Leaning against the doorway of the boys' room, I watched them for a few moments. It would probably be good for them to be with their dad. But dammit, Corey, why you gotta take my boys? I started to tear up and decided I'd better walk out before one of them woke up and saw creepy mama stalking them.

I went back downstairs and turned on the news at a low volume. Sighing, I wondered why I didn't have my oldest do the dishes; she was always getting out of her chores. I was sleepy, but I couldn't go to bed with a junky kitchen. If Julian woke up in the middle of the night to find it messy, I would never hear the end of it. He hated a dirty kitchen, and I hated waking up to it, too. Once I started, it actually didn't take long. I shut everything down, turned off the lights, and dragged my weary body up the steps.

As I approached the bedroom door, I could hear Julian snoring. Moving quietly through the darkness, I slipped into the master bathroom to take a shower and get ready for bed. Afterward, I grabbed my Bath and Body Works lotion to moisturize my body. I inhaled the sweet scent of Japanese Cherry Blossom; I always made sure to smell good before bed.

Sliding in between the sheets, I settled down, figuring Julian was out cold. But then he grabbed me by the waist and pulled me closer, insisting on spooning with me every night for his own comfort.

But tonight, he had more on his mind. I felt his warm kisses trailing down my neck and his hands roaming over my body. I knew what this meant. His lips made a slow journey into my cleavage, ensuring each breast received attention. I felt my nipples respond to his tantalizing tongue, sending sparks through me. He teased his way down my stomach, lingering on every inch of my flesh until he hovered at the soft hairline of my most intimate area.

Building the anticipation, he looked up at me with the lust in his eyes, and I knew he could sense my desire. *Please! Eat me now! Devour these goodies!* I thought, nearly breathless. I could hardly stand it.

Finally, Julian dove into my slit, devouring me like it was his last meal on death row. The pleasure built to an almost unbearable level, and I struggled to hold back my climax. I wanted him to keep going, but dammit, I couldn't help it. Moans escaped my lips as I grabbed his head, pressing him deeper into my sweetness. "I love you!" I whispered as I exploded in his mouth. He drank every drop, kissing my lower lips to savor the moment.

"I love when you come to bed smelling good," he whispered, his voice thick with desire.

"I see... I thought you were mad at me," I giggled, catching my breath.

"I was, but then you smelled so fuckin' good, I couldn't help it," he said, flashing a sinister grin.

"Well, maybe I need to make you mad all the time." I rolled on top of him, taking control, and began to suck his rod like I was freestyling on a mic. His eyes rolled back in pleasure, and he moaned as I tried to take him deeper. I could feel him pulsating in my mouth, his rod growing harder with every passing second. Just as he was about to explode, he turned me back over, forcing himself into my wet hole, and we began to fuck like crazy.

"Ladye, I'm about to cum," Julian moaned.

"Cum for me, baby. Fill me up!" I urged, grabbing his ass to drive him deeper inside me.

"I'm cumming; this feels so good," he whimpered. I could feel his rod throbbing harder, pounding faster against me until he let out a loud cry and slumped over, surrendering to the pleasure. Just like that, I had conquered Rome. He rested his full weight on top of me, his manhood still inside me. I felt my walls tighten around him, and every time they did, he jumped, riding out the waves of ecstasy until it finally subsided, and he rolled off.

"Goodnight, Ladye," he whispered, his breath warm against my skin.

"Goodnight, Julian." I scooted into a spooning position, and we fell asleep peacefully, as if we hadn't wanted to kill each other just hours before. It felt like nothing had even happened.

When my alarm clock went off at six the next morning, I quickly silenced it to avoid waking Julian. He looked so sweet and sexy, lying next to me, his eyelashes fluttering gently in his sleep. The temptation to stay under the covers was strong, but I had to get up for work.

Thursdays were always my early days, a trade-off for not being there on the weekends. I saved Saturdays and Sundays for family time and my trips to Houston. As Ladye, I loved being with my kids, who were always involved in something—whether it was basketball or cheerleading. This weekend would be my alter ego's turn, and as Chanelle, I enjoyed flying off to another state, diving into a whole 'nother world. I felt a little like Beyoncé when she channeled her other personality, Sasha Fierce.

I pulled down the covers and quietly swung my legs over the edge of the bed, trying to sneak out. I inched my way over bit by bit, holding my breath, but of course, my plan didn't unfold as expected.

"What are you doing?" Julian rolled over, throwing his arm over me. I tried to squirm free, but he held tight, scooting closer to cuddle.

"I have to go to the salon, baby. I need to be there by seven to open the doors. I can't be late."

Memoirs of an Invisible Woman

"You can't be a little late? Aww, come on! I had plans for you this morning," he said, tossing the covers back over me.

"While I'd love to spend my entire day in bed with you, honey, I have a business to run and a family to take care of. Lying under these covers with you is not an option today." He relaxed his grip, and I seized the moment to jump out of bed. Snatching my clothes for the day, I dashed to the bathroom to take a shower.

As I settled in under the warm water, I whispered my morning prayers, thanking God for His many blessings. I knew the man upstairs was looking out for me. I had so much to be grateful for, and I tried to carve out time to praise Him, even when I was in a hurry.

As I whispered my amens, I noticed a figure approaching through the frosted glass. Julian swung open the shower door, buck-naked, stepping in with a grin. We hadn't showered together in a long time, but today was not the day for that.

"Julian, I really have to be on time. I can't play with you this morning. It's already 6:15, and I need to be out of here by 6:45..." I tried to sound tough, but his gentle caresses sent shivers down my spine. Oh my, that felt good. "So, fooling around is not in the plans today!"

"Okay, Ladye, have it your way," he whispered, nibbling on my earlobes and wrapping his arms around me to cup my breasts. "You smell like heaven."

"Yeah, and you're about to make me catch hell if I'm late!" I sighed, leaning back against his chest and allowing him to tease my aroused peaks.

"You won't be late, baby, I promise," Julian replied, then he turned me around, sinking to his knees to go downtown. I watched the water stream down my legs and over his head as his tongue flicked in and out of my swollen mound. I nearly went cross-eyed with ecstasy; it felt so amazing.

"Oh my God, Julian, please stop," I begged, struggling to maintain my resolve.

"I'll stop as soon as you cum in my mouth so I can taste you and start my day," he replied, talking, breathing, and savoring me all at once. (He was a very talented man.) I knew we were at the point of no return, and trying to fight him off would be futile—and honestly, a little foolish. So, I closed my eyes, relaxed, and surrendered to my man.

After I released my essence into his mouth, Julian stepped back so I could finish my shower. I wanted to prolong the moment, but the clock was ticking.

I washed up quickly, then jumped out of the shower to apply lotion. After slipping into black leggings, a black button-down shirt, and some jewelry, I slid on my comfortable shoes. I always left my work shoes at the salon. As I walked through the bedroom, I caught my reflection in the full-length mirror.

"Oh shoot, I forgot to brush my teeth!" I hurried back to the bathroom, grabbing my toothbrush and toothpaste. Once I finished, I smiled at myself in the mirror, giving myself the "you are so beautiful" affirmation.

Zipping out of the bedroom, I headed straight for the front door. "Baby, can you please make sure the kids get up and out on time? I didn't make their lunches last night, so can you give them money for lunch?" I called, just as I was about to walk out.

"Oh hell, where are my keys?"

"Ladye, your keys are on the kitchen counter!" he yelled back.

Cursing under my breath, I turned around and sprinted to the kitchen, where Julian was busy making breakfast. I grabbed my keys and leaned over to give him a quick kiss. "I love you just for being you," I said, smiling.

We exchanged a big kiss before I rushed out the door.

"Call me when you get to work, please! I love you!" he shouted after me.

Finally, out of the house and into the car, I glanced at the clock on the dash: 6:47. Yes! I'm going to make it—thank you, Jesus. The thought, combined with the incredible shower experience, put a huge grin on my face as I sang along with the radio and drove away.

Chapter Seven

I pulled up to the salon just as the sun began to rise. It was a little chilly this time of year, but the silky waves of violet, blue, yellow, and orange in the sky made up for it. It was an inspiring start to what was sure to be another beautiful day.

I parked next to a cute purple Jeep Wrangler, which belonged to Robert—Rob for short. Well, he's here early! As I stepped out of my truck, grabbed my things, and made my way to the back door of the salon, I reflected on how it all began. Rob had been with me since I opened the shop 16 years ago. I was 18, and he was 21, both fresh out of cosmetology school. After receiving a settlement from an accident I had as a kid, I decided to open my own hair salon, and Rob joined me. There had been good times and bad, but we never looked back. Rob made my life so much easier; we'd been friends for years, so he really understood me—my likes, my dislikes, and how I wanted to run the salon.

As I opened the door, I heard gospel music playing throughout the building. Now, I know Rob ain't playing no gospel music—he's a heathen! I was convinced it wasn't possible, but sure enough, Rob was playing Kirk Franklin.

"Good morning, Robert," I whispered as I approached the salon floor. He already had a client in his chair, and I didn't want to startle them.

"Hey, Ms. Ladye! How are you, beautiful?"

"I'm well, thanks for asking. I'm not complaining, but what's with the music? It's not your style."

"My partner is into gospel right now, and my clients seem to like it. When they're happy, they tip more," he grinned.

"Okay, that makes sense. But why are you here so early? I'm used to being here by myself for at least another two hours," I smiled.

"I know I have a crazy weekend coming up, and for some reason, that little new girl Kita you hired to be the damn receptionist double-booked some of my clients. You'd think the little chicken would know how to use a computer and set appointments properly, but I guess not. Good help is hard to find nowadays!" He tried to sound tough but burst out laughing. "C'mon, Brenda, let me get your relaxer started." He motioned to another client waiting for her turn.

"Rob, don't do Kita like that! She's still learning the ropes, and she's only 18. We have to be patient with her. I think she's going to work out fine; we just need to teach her the ropes, just like someone had to teach your ass to stop being so messy and clean up after yourself!" I teased.

"Ohhhhhh no, you didn't, Ms. Ladye! Was that shade or was that a read?" he smirked.

"It was a little of both." We both put up our dukes and pretended to fight.

"How many clients do you have today?" I asked, playfully shoving him aside.

"I think about 15, but most of them are relaxers. I have two sew-ins scheduled, but for the most part, I should be good on time. You know I love a busy day because then we get all the gossip for the week."

"Yeah, I have a full day too. Remember, I leave in the morning, so I need you to hold down the fort."

"Like I always do," he sighed dramatically. "I have to do everything around here."

"Oh, shut up, you fool. Get to work!" I slapped him on the butt—something I'm allowed to do because we're friends, and he's gay. Of course, even if he weren't, I'd still want to touch that ass. At 6'4", 230 pounds, with curly hair and light skin, he was fine as hell. I laughed every time a female client hit on him; their faces dropped when he informed them of his sexual preference. It was hilarious.

Memoirs of an Invisible Woman

If he were straight, I knew this shop would be lit up with women fighting over him. Dudes were already squabbling for his attention. They were always lined up to see him—gay, straight, bi, trans; they all loved him. The drama he brought to the table was priceless entertainment. He dressed impeccably, and every five minutes, a package arrived at the salon for him. We're talking flowers, candy, jewelry, purses, clothes—anything you can think of, these guys were spoiling him rotten. Seriously.

Rob had been with his partner for about ten years, and I loved their relationship because they never tried to hide anything. They figured people would either accept them or not; either way, they had solid jobs and were still getting paid.

"Is everybody coming in today, Ladye?" Rob asked.

"As far as I know, the crew should be arriving between 9:00 and 10:00, as usual. You know Thursday is usually the start of the turn-up weekend, so everyone's day should be full and interesting."

"It's gonna be cray-cray!" he yelled.

"Did you make sure the refrigerator is stocked for the day, Rob?"

"Yes, I sure did! There's plenty of pop, water, and wine to last the whole day and then some. You know I'm on my job, baby," he beamed.

"Thank you, honey, because you do stay on it!" I teased.

"Oooooook!" He snapped his fingers and walked into the shampoo room just as my client walked in.

"Hey, Trish! How's it going, girl?" I asked.

"It's going, girl; I can't complain," she replied.

"Are you getting the usual?"

"I'm not sure if I need a relaxer; can you check for me?"

"Of course!" I went to the computer and punched in Trish's name. "Trish, it's been eight weeks. Do you want to do it today?"

"Yes, please! My hair is so nappy."

I sat Trish in my chair. She was an executive assistant for a major company but was down-to-earth.

"Girl, your hair is not all that nappy, but you do need a touch-up." I started to base her hair with a sensitive scalp cream before applying the relaxer.

"So, how have you been, Ladye?" Trish asked.

"Girl, same old, same old—trying to make it in this crazy world without losing my mind. It's been a chaotic month, but I'm working. All I do is keep praying and trying to maintain my sanity before I lose it," I said, shaking my head.

"Girl, you're preaching to the choir! Life pushes you around sometimes. You just gotta do what you gotta do."

"C'mon, Trish. Let me rinse this relaxer out of your hair and get you shampooed and conditioned. I know your schedule is busy, and you don't want to be here with me all day." I rinsed her relaxer, shampooed her, and then sat her under the dryer with her treatment. By then, it was time for my next client, and I heard the door open right on time. I hoped the day would go smoothly like this all day.

Reem Denise

Chapter Eight

"Ladye, phone's for you!" Rob yelled from across the room.

I had just finished a shampoo and wiped my hands on a towel as I walked to the front counter. When I picked up the phone, a sexy voice greeted me.

"Hello, gorgeous," said Julian. "How's your day going, Ms. Monroe?"

"Hi, baby! It's going good so far. What about yours? Did the kids get off to school alright?"

"Of course they did, baby. Remmie is with my mom today because they're going to the mall to do some shopping. She said she wanted to buy her some earrings. And she's taking Corey and Jewels this weekend to get them some stuff she's been promising." One thing I loved about Julian's family is that since the day we decided to be a couple, they treated all my kids the same and never showed any favoritism. His parents were especially good at that; if they did for one, they did for all. Nana and Poppi never missed a birthday. The kids were just as crazy about them, and vice versa.

"Oh, that's cool! The girls will love that because your mom goes crazy when she takes them shopping!" I laughed.

"I know! I told her, please don't buy Remmie anything else; there's nowhere to put it, and she's not getting a bigger room," Julian said.

"Did you decide what you want for dinner?" I asked.

"The kids want pizza and wings, and I figure, why not? I'll grab it on the way home because I'm sure I'll be done before you. If we left dinner up to you on a Thursday, we'd starve."

"Stop it, Julian," I sighed. "I'm trying to get out by six because I want to spend time with y'all before I leave tomorrow."

"We'll see, Ladye; we'll see." I tried to ignore the sarcasm in his voice.

"Okay, my client is ready, and I have another one waiting, so I'll call you on my lunch break. Love you, babe."

"Love you more, Ladye."

Before I could walk back to my client, Rob called my name again.

"Robert, why are you yelling? I'm right across from you, and I'm sure you don't want to be that loud about anything that isn't important, you jerk," I scolded.

"Actually, I had to ask you a question about you and Julian." I was not impressed with his smug grin.

"Tread lightly, Rob. You know how I am about my fucking personal life and my business life not mixing, so let's not fall out about Julian," I said, giving him the side eye.

"Girl, please! Ain't nobody scared of you or those silly faces you try to make like you're intimidating somebody. My question is, how do you stay with the same dick year after year, after motherfucking year? That shit has to get boring!"

"Rob, please know I hate you. To answer your question, yes, it does get boring, but we do a lot to spice it up. Nine times out of ten, it's only boring when you make it boring. Julian and I fuck all the time, and we role-play. Because of the love we have for each other, it never really gets boring; it's what we make it."

"Soooo! Ms. Ladye, do you think Julian ever cheated on you?" Rob's client, Mercedes, piped up, popping her gum. I didn't like the fact that she was the second person in two days to ask that question. What is wrong with these people? Why are they so interested in me and Julian?

"First of all, I'm sure he has cheated because I don't put shit past no man," I said, standing in the middle of the salon with my hands on my hips. "Second of all, if he did, it would have never come to my business or my home, so I could care less. Julian is a lot of things; stupid isn't one of them. He would never let a bitch near me or even know who I was. Julian protects his family at all costs."

I walked over to Rob's station and looked down at his client. "Third and final thing, Mercedes, stop popping that fucking gum in my salon before I put your ratchet ass out. You see the fucking sign; it says clear as day, no popping of gum!" I really did have a sign because I hated that shit and always believed it was incredibly ignorant.

"Well, damn, Ladye, I guess you told me," she said, sitting up straight and saluting me. I ought to knock her the fuck out, but kicking a client's ass is not a good look.

"Oh, bitch, she is real sensitive about Julian's ass," Rob whispered to his client like I couldn't hear him as I walked away.

"Stop playing with me, Rob, before I punch you in the head!" I threw a towel across the room, trying to hit him with it.

"Oh no, you didn't! Why are you always throwing stuff at me?" he hollered.

"Because I can't reach you, and you're a smart ass!"

"Ladye, you know I love you!" Rob ran over and tried to hug me.

"Get off of me, boy!" I slapped him away, pretending to be mad but screaming with delight. Finally, he got his big arms around me and pulled me in for a mushy hug and a kiss on the cheek.

"Agh! I got slimed!" I yelled. "Okay, okay, we gotta get back to work! We have a long day, and I can't play with you people anymore! Some of us don't have sugar daddies to take care of us," I laughed.

"I don't have no sugar daddy, bitch; I just have a daddy!" Rob bragged.

Everyone settled down, giving me a moment to hear myself think as I chuckled.

"Good morning, everybody!" said Shamika as she walked into the salon, waving and smiling like she always does. She had only worked for me for about six months, but she was killing it with business. There were a couple of weeks when she made more than I did. This little chick was all about her paper, and I loved it. She didn't turn a client down and was good at what she did. Plus, I admired her spirit. She was a young girl with an old soul, probably because her grandparents raised her. She was so respectful and quickly made a name for herself, earning our respect in no time. The fact that she was Julian's niece didn't even factor in.

"Morning, Mika!" I called out.

"Well, look who's coming in on time today," Rob said, turning to her.

"Rob, shut up! It's too early for your shit, and besides, I'm always on time because I'm here before my clients," Mika clapped back at him. As the second lead stylist, she had every right to.

"You're right, Ms. Mika, you are so right!" Rob bowed dramatically to the winner of that match. Mika sauntered to her station; head held high like the queen of the court. She had such a genuine personality and was always positive. Despite goofing around with Rob, she was excellent at keeping the salon drama-free. Mika was a glass-half-full type of person and very non-confrontational. Her humble spirit reminded me a lot of Julian's mother; you could tell she raised Mika because she was his mom all over again. She was like a breath of fresh air when she came into the salon.

She was a stunning caramel-colored girl with long hair she always wore straight, parted in the middle. Standing at about 5'7", her shape was poppin', but let her tell it, she was so fat. Now, I'll admit Mika loved to eat, but she wasn't fat at all—just thick in all the right spots.

"Mika, how many clients do you have today?" I asked.

"About four sew-ins. Why, what's up?"

"I was wondering if you felt like doing my sew-in later because I have to catch a plane early in the morning."

"Oh, no problem, Ladye! I'll wait around until you're finished. I got you. How do you want it done?"

"I just want it straight with a part on the side, probably about 24 inches. I have some bundle hair in the storage room I wanted to try."

Of course, Rob had to butt in, as usual. "Oh, my gawd, Ladye! You and that side part—I'm so sick of that look on you! Do something different, please!"

"Rob, was I talking to you? I didn't think so, so stay out of my business." I put my hand up, my palm turned out, and walked away from him, shaking my head and tuning out his cackling.

I started working on my client while I thought about Mika. I'd been in her life since she was six years old when Julian and I started dating. Her mother brought her over to Julian's mom's house one day to stay the weekend and never returned. Sometimes, I felt like it was the best thing for Mika because they all spoiled her to death and made sure she had the best of everything. I was like her auntie/big sister, and we could talk about anything because she knew she could trust me not to tell Julian anything we discussed. Mika had a good head on her shoulders and mostly stayed out of trouble, following whatever advice I gave her.

"Ladye," she called out.

"Yes, Mik?"

"Remmie was at the house this morning talking my ear off," she giggled. "Soon as Grandma told her I was home, she busted into my room and wouldn't shut up! All I could do was laugh because Poppi was like, 'Oh gawd, Remmie done got a hold of Shamika, and she ain't gone let go.' Ladye, I went to take a shower, and she came in right behind me, sat on the toilet, and kept talking while I was showering. Grandma told her to come out of the bathroom, and she said, 'Grandma, I'm trying to talk to Mika because I need to tell her about my life because I never see her.' She followed me into my room, and when I told her I had to get dressed for work, she said, 'It's okay, Mika, I'll turn my back like I do Mommy, and I can just keep talking while you get dressed.' It was hilarious because she really turned her back while I got dressed, and as soon as I was finished, she turned right back around and kept talking to me."

"That sounds like Remmie," I smiled. "She is something else. It's gotten to the point where I just let her talk because she's going to regardless."

"You are absolutely right." We both cracked up.

"My dad came over yesterday and gave me some money. I just took it and put it on my dresser. He thinks I'm still sixteen and needs to give me an allowance. He comes over every week and hands me $300. I just put it in the bank because I don't need it; I just stack it."

"You better! Good for you. You know you're daddy's little girl, and he'll give you the world if you ask him."

"I know! Sometimes I hate being an only child, but then Remmie comes over, and everything becomes clear. I'm okay with being the only one because I can't imagine having a little sister like her," she chuckled.

"You might have gotten a sister like Corey or Jewels," I teased.

"I don't think my dad wanted to chance it."

"You might be right. But leave my baby alone; I know she's a handful, but it's because all of you guys are way older than she is. I think she has an old soul like you because she wants to be like y'all."

"I guess you're right, L, but Remmie is a trip!"

Her first client arrived, and I went to get mine from under the dryer to take out her rollers and style her hair. Everyone was quiet again—for the moment—but I knew that wouldn't last. Honestly, I looked forward to it all; I really loved having my own business.

Chapter Nine

"Ladye, while you're away, I think I'm going to make some changes and do a little redecorating," said Rob.

"Oh really?" I looked him up and down like he was a creepy, crawly insect with 20 legs. "Mika! This nigga right here, doing all these damn relaxers like he's on an assembly line, and now he thinks he's in charge!"

"Mm-hmm," she said, shaking her head. "That boy is too big for his britches. Thinks he's all that and a bag of chips."

"First of all, no one says that anymore, Ms. Mika," Rob retorted, sticking his tongue out at her as she rolled her eyes. "Second, Ladye, I hate my station across from yours. I want to be right next to you so I can read your thoughts, bitch!"

"Well, first off, you ain't changing shit! Don't make me laugh," I said. "Second, you're fine over there, because we could never sit that close and actually work. Not to mention, we both gotta be by the door in case some hood chick comes up in here, and we gotta lock her ass in!"

"You know what, L, you're right. We will lock a bitch in and beat that ass if she tries it in here! Now, she can go down to Brown Sugar with that mess, but if she comes in here with that shit, she's getting her ass beat!" Rob snapped his fingers and strutted off.

I glanced toward the door and saw what looked like five dozen roses, with a pair of skinny legs in a short skirt and five-inch stilettos sticking out from under them. Kita peeked around the bundle and smiled. She was still a little shy and new at her job, but she was a pretty little thing.

"Good morning, everybody," she said softly. "These were out front. There were so many, I couldn't see a card." Kita set the roses on the counter and searched through them some more.

"They're probably for Rob's annoying ass," I groaned, walking toward the shampoo room. "He probably met a nigga, and now we're going to have flowers stinking up my damn shop for the next few weeks. Thanks a lot, Rob."

Rob walked over to smell the flowers, and Kita handed him the card. He read it, and a wide smirk spread across his face.

"Oh, bitch! These are actually for you, not me at all."

"What? Stop teasing me," I said, walking up to the front. He handed me the card and leaned back, waiting for my reaction.

To the most beautiful lady I have ever laid my eyes on, Ladye Monroe. From your secret crush!!

"Wait, who the hell is sending me flowers? And who is my secret crush?" I looked around, and everyone was watching me and snickering. "Y'all are weird! I know they're from Julian." I walked back to my station, pretending that it didn't matter, even though it did. Because if they aren't from Julian, I'm going to be in big trouble.

Towards the end of the day, the salon finally started to quiet down. I said goodbye to my last client, and Rob was finishing up his. I figured Mika was in the break room, probably eating, because I smelled food. I saw Kita closing out the books for the day. As I walked over to the desk and glanced at the roses, I wondered who in the world could have sent them. I hated roses, and Julian knew that, so it couldn't have been him. Not to mention, he was maybe twenty percent romantic, and sending flowers was just not his style.

"Kita, how did we do today?" I asked.

"We did pretty well, L. We cleared $15,843.62 for the day. This weekend is going to be busy, so we should be good."

"That's great! Now make sure you hold down the fort while I'm gone, but let Rob think he's running this shit by himself so he can feel like the boss!"

"Okay, L, I got it," Kita said, winking at me.

"Ladye, are you ready for me to start your hair?" Mika asked as she came out of the break room.

"Yes, ma'am." I gladly sat down in her chair. I loved styling, but it was nice to just relax and let someone else work their magic on my hair.

"You might as well head to the bowl because I need to shampoo your hair, and you need a treatment—you haven't had one in, what, six months?" Mika grabbed a towel and headed to the back.

"Six months, Mika? You sure?" I asked, following her.

"Yes, I'm sure. You need one today." I leaned back in the chair as she shampooed my hair. She applied the treatment, then sat me under the dryer. As I sat there under the heat, I kept looking at the roses, racking my brain for the answer to my so-called secret crush. I wasn't into mushy drama; I hated soap opera stuff. But now I was being pulled into a mystery I didn't have the time—or desire—for.

I never talked to anyone in Cincinnati, nor did I give off a vibe like I wanted to talk to anyone in Houston. I was friendly with people, but never flirtatious. So, who's watching me, being weird and shit? Mika finished my hair with a perfect sew-in, and as usual, she nailed it. I wasn't surprised at all.

"So, who sent you the flowers?" she asked. "Because I know my uncle didn't. He doesn't have a romantic bone in his body."

"Honestly, Mika, I have no idea. I thought the same thing, but I don't know anyone who would send me flowers. Anyone who knows me knows I hate the smell of them. I'm so confused about it. Please don't mention this to him or anyone in the family, though—I don't need the drama from Julian."

"I got your back," she reassured me. "I'd never mention what happens in the shop to my family. My uncle's cool as hell, but he's also a little crazy. I know how he gets when he's jealous. One time, Uncle John said you had a fat ass, and Uncle Julian almost ripped his head off. Grandma had to step in and stop him!"

"Really? No way! I've never heard that story," I said, completely thrown off. What the hell is going on today?

"Yep! It was crazy, scary, and funny all at the same time because none of us knew Uncle Julian was going to react like that. Well, Grandma knew, 'cause she knows her sons. As soon as Uncle John said it, Grandma looked at him and asked why he'd say something like that. Uncle Julian grabbed his neck so fast and started squeezing, saying, 'Don't look at her again or I'll kill you.' We were all scared. Grandma told Julian to let him go, or she was going to choke him herself! So, he let go, and Uncle John fell to the floor gasping for air. Poppi was laughing and said, 'You're gonna learn about talking about people's women!' Uncle Julian just grabbed Jewels and walked out."

"When was this?"

"A few years ago. Remmie wasn't born yet."

I was floored. Julian had never told me any of this. I guess he didn't want me to know how protective he was, even back then. But I knew the moment we kissed that he loved me. I sighed, feeling happy, and got back to cleaning up my station.

Around eight that evening, I finally left the shop.

"Y'all please lock up for me! I'll see y'all Monday afternoon, or better yet, Tuesday. Love y'all!"

I walked out the back door, my mind drifting to Julian and bedroom fantasies. Suddenly, I stopped dead in the middle of the sidewalk, a shiver running down my spine like someone had walked over my grave. I glanced around the parking lot—empty, except for a couple of cars, with the only light coming from a lone streetlamp. Why am I being so paranoid?

"This is ridiculous! I'm outta here," I muttered, trying to sound confident, but my voice wavered. I took a deep breath, forcing myself to walk calmly toward my Jeep. *I'm just tired. It's been a long day.*

As I got in, something caught my eye—a piece of paper stuck under my windshield wiper. I snatched it and held it up under the interior light.

"Hi."

That's all it said. And that's all it took to make my heart race. My nerves were shot, and I quickly slammed the door shut, feeling freaked out. I hated weird, cryptic shit like this. Who the hell was watching me? I shoved the key into the ignition, popped in a Michael Jackson CD, and peeled out of there, heading straight home.

Reem Denise

Chapter Ten

When I pulled into my driveway just before nine that evening, I was surprised to find the house completely dark. *What the hell?* I'd be lucky to see all the lights off by eleven, much less as early as nine.

I entered through the side door, marveling at the silence and was even more impressed by the spotless kitchen. No one was in the living room, and even the big screen TV—usually blaring ninety percent of the time—was off.

Reem Denise

"Anyone here?" I whispered, but the only answer was silence. I slipped off my shoes and headed upstairs. A faint light glowed beneath Corey's door, so I knocked lightly and stepped inside. She was curled up on her bed, watching TV.

"Hey, Corey Boo, what're you watching?"

"The Cosby Show," she yawned. "Then I'm going to bed. I had a long day."

"What about the rest of my crew?" I asked.

"Mom, you're not gonna believe this! They're all asleep. Julian took us out for pizza and ice cream. The little ones got tired, we came home, took showers, and they were knocked out!" She shook her head, amazed.

"That's awesome! Sounds like you guys had a good time. You know I'm leaving in the morning for the weekend, right?"

"Yes, ma'am, I know. We're going to Grandma's. I think Poppi's picking us up from school since Julian doesn't get off until five. He didn't want us home by ourselves that long."

"Okay, sounds good. I love you, pretty girl! See you Sunday morning. Never forget how much I love you. Corey, you're my first friend, my first smile, my first cup of tea."

I got up to leave, blowing her a kiss because she said she was too old for them now. She pretended to ignore me, but I knew she loved me back.

I went into the rest of the bedrooms, and sure enough, everyone else was snoozing like little angels. It was easy to see them that way when they were asleep. I smiled, whispering a prayer over each of them.

Finally, I headed to my own room, expecting it to be pitch black and bracing myself for Julian's snores. But when I opened the door, I froze. There were candles—lit, flickering candles—everywhere. Their flames reflected in the dresser mirror, dancing seductively to the soft, soulful sounds of Etta James

I turned to see Julian lounging against the pillows, the silky sheet draped across his lap, his chiseled chest gleaming with baby oil. The room was thick with the scent of his favorite cologne, Issey Miyake, a fragrance that always made my head spin—it was like heaven had been bottled. His hands were behind his head, naturally flexing his biceps as his eyes roved over me. Slowly, he licked his lips, then bit his bottom one, sending heat through my body.

"Hey, baby," he said softly.

I walked over to the bed, leaned down, and kissed him deeply. "Hi, baby," I sighed.

"Your bath water's ready," he said, gently nudging me away.

"But... Julian, baby, I want you now," I pouted.

"No, I want to do this right. Go take a bath so I can take care of you before you hop on that plane. I'm gonna miss you all weekend, as usual. And I'm gonna make sure you miss me too."

I pouted again, sticking out my tongue before heading to the bathroom. He was right; it would feel better after I washed up. As I slipped into the steaming Jacuzzi tub, I tried to relax, but my mind wouldn't stop racing.

Why does it always have to be this double life? I thought, sinking deeper into the water. But I had goals. I wanted that mansion for my babies, and I needed to stack as much paper as I could before this whole jig was up. That was the scariest part—knowing that if Julian ever found out, it would be over. No second chances. No coming back.

Still, the risk felt worth it. I needed to make sure my family was set. And I was good at covering my tracks. Pash always had my back, sending me fake itineraries from a bogus email with seminars and events where I was listed as a speaker. I hated being so sneaky, but I was in too deep to stop now.

The fast money was hard to resist. I could pull in over $5,000 in just one weekend as one of the most requested dancers at the club. And I didn't have to worry about anyone finding out because I worked in a whole different time zone, far from the prying eyes of coworkers, teachers, friends, and family. Plus, the club had assigned me my own bodyguard, Jay, who never let anyone get too close when I was on stage. I was well protected.

I leaned back in the hot, soapy water, trying to let the tension seep out of my muscles. But I was careful not to get my hair wet—couldn't have that before the weekend even started. Just as I closed my eyes and stretched, letting my fingers drift between my legs, the door flew open.

I thrashed about in the tub until I managed to grab onto the side of the Jacuzzi. Looking up sheepishly, I saw Julian standing at the entrance, his face caught between hilarity and confusion.

"Uh, I was just checking to see if you're almost done," he said, raising one eyebrow. "Are you okay?"

"You scared the hell out of me, Julian!" I snapped, but my voice trembled with a mixture of surprise and laughter.

"Practicing some synchronized swimming or something?" he teased.

"Shut up!"

"I'll give it an eight—five for artistic impression, and three for technical difficulty."

"Get out, you ass!" I giggled, chucking my loofah at him. "I'll be out in a minute!"

He ducked out of the bathroom, but I could still hear him laughing as I hurried to finish. I wanted to join him in bed, craving the warmth of his touch.

Trying to be sneaky, I slipped out of the tub and tiptoed toward the bed. But before I could even reach the step stool, Julian grabbed me, pulling me into his arms and kissing me passionately. I barely had a chance to catch my breath as he explored my body with his hands. He kissed my neck, my shoulders, then trailed his lips between my breasts, pausing here and there as if savoring each inch of me.

He knelt down in front of me, his lips moving to my stomach, while his hands massaged my ass. Lifting me effortlessly, he laid me on the chaise at the foot of our bed, spreading my legs open with a mischievous grin.

Julian's tongue flicked over my clit, sending waves of pleasure coursing through my body. I gasped, my body responding involuntarily, arching toward him. The sensation was overwhelming, toeing the line between too much and not enough. I wanted him to stop, but at the same time, I never wanted him to stop.

"Oh God, Julian!" I cried, as I grabbed his head, pulling him closer. He hummed against me, the vibrations intensifying everything. I bucked and squirmed as he lapped up my juices, pushing me over the edge. I couldn't hold back, and I climaxed, my body convulsing in bliss.

Catching my breath, I flipped him onto the bed, straddling him as I rode him hard. He moaned, his hands gripping my hips, lost in the moment.

"Ladye, please... I'm going to cum," he groaned, his voice thick with need.

"I want you to," I panted, my body moving faster. "Cum all over me."

"Ladye... it's too much!" His voice rose, struggling to keep quiet.

"Shut up before you wake the kids," I growled playfully. "Take it like a champ, the way I take that rod!"

With a final groan, Julian released himself, his body trembling beneath mine as he came hard. I collapsed on top of him, both of us breathless, and that's how we fell asleep—entangled in each other, spent and satisfied.

Reem Denise

Chapter Eleven

I woke up at four in the morning, mad as hell that Pash booked us this early-ass flight. What the hell was she thinking? We had to be at the airport by 5:30, and just getting out of bed felt like pure agony.

Julian groaned lazily beside me, his arms reaching out to wrap around my waist. "Do you gotta go?" he whispered, his voice still thick with sleep.

"Yes, sir," I whimpered, turning toward him. Grabbing his handsome face, I kissed every inch of it, ending on those delicious lips. "Pash will be here by 4:45. I gotta hop in the shower and get myself together."

Reem Denise

Reluctantly, I climbed out of bed and trudged toward the bathroom. God, I just wanted to lie there with Julian, but duty called. I had obligations to tend to. As I closed the bathroom door behind me, my phone rang.

"Hello?" I didn't even bother hiding the irritation in my voice.

"Good morning, bestie! Are you up?" Pash's cheerful voice chirped through the line. She was like one of those Disney princesses who woke up with birds chirping around her and forest animals singing a happy tune.

"Yes, I'm up, about to take a shower. See you in a minute. Don't call me back—it's too early for this shit. Bye, Pash." Who gets up at four in the morning? Who even *talks* at four in the morning?

"Well damn, I never! Bye, Ladye. See you in a few!" she said, still sounding annoyingly chipper. There was definitely something wrong with her.

I loved my friend, but I was furious about being up so early just to catch a flight that was barely two and a half hours long. We could've flown out at noon and been just fine. But of course, Pash always had to be on the first flight—knowing damn well it worked my nerves. She enjoyed pulling stunts like this.

Sighing, I turned on the shower, rinsed my face, and brushed my teeth while I waited for the water to heat up. Catching my reflection in the mirror, I recited my daily affirmations.

"I am beautiful.

I am a strong woman.

I am who God says I am, and the only person who can change that is me."

I smiled at myself, gave a quick wink, and stepped into the shower. As the warm water hit my skin, I closed my eyes and began to pray.

"Father God, in the mighty and matchless name of Your son Jesus, I thank You for another day. Father, forgive me for my sins—those of commission and omission. I ask that You protect my family and watch over them while I'm away. Lord, I know it is in You that

I move, live, and have my being, and I thank You for being everything to me. I praise You in Jesus' name. Amen."

When I got out of the bathroom, Julian was already out of bed. I hoped he was downstairs making coffee. I quickly threw on a sweatsuit; it was the most comfortable way to travel, easy to get dressed in, and a breeze when going through the metal detectors. Rushing downstairs, I was relieved to see him holding a steaming cup of java.

"Hey, I brought your bag down for you," he said, handing me my drink.

"I see. Thank you for always making sure I'm good, baby," I replied, taking a grateful sip.

"I always will, Ladye," he said, planting a sweet kiss on my cheek. "I hope you have fun this weekend. Don't let Pash get you in any trouble."

"She won't, babe. I have too much to do to fool with Pash," I laughed just as my cell phone vibrated on the table.

"I'm outside, grumpy ass," Pash teased through the line.

"Okay, I'm coming! Let me go kiss my babies goodbye. I'll be out in two minutes." I dashed up to the kids' rooms, planting soft kisses on each of their foreheads. I needed to hurry and get out of there to put all my plans into action. These trips were for them, but being away broke my heart. They needed me around all the time. Wiping away a few stray tears, I sprinted back downstairs.

As I grabbed my bag and headed for the door, I leaned in to give Julian a goodbye kiss. He held the door open, watching me walk toward Pash's rental car.

"Hold on a minute!" I yelled, racing back into the house. "Don't forget the boys' basketball game! And make sure Remmie doesn't get locked out of the bathroom. Oh, and tell Corey—"

"Ladye! Calm down!" Julian chuckled, a warm smile on his face. "We've got it under control."

"Okay, okay, I gotta go!" I said, turning back toward the car, but just as I was about to get in, another thought struck me.

"Julian! Make sure you get more milk!" I dashed back to him and threw my arms around his neck. He bent down for a long, passionate kiss that made my heart race. "Shit! I gotta go!"

I hopped into the car, waving as I blew him a kiss before closing the door. Pash revved the engine, and we pulled away, leaving Julian behind.

Oh, I love them so much! I'm missing them already! What are they going to do without me? I started to have a pity party in my head when Pash interrupted.

"Are y'all's goodbyes always so dramatic? I mean, it feels like we just did a whole *Gone With the Wind* moment or something. I don't know nothin' 'bout birthin' no babies!" she said in a southern drawl. "Bitch, that was too much for a weekend trip!"

"Shut up, bitch!" I knew she was teasing me. "Dang, we love each other, and we miss each other when we're apart!"

"Right, bitch, right! And what do you mean you don't know anything about birthing babies? You do know you have two sons, right?" I looked confused.

"Yes, bitch, I know I have two sons, but I didn't birth them; they cut those fuckers out of me," she laughed. This girl really works my last nerve, I promise you.

When we turned in the rental at the airport, the man at the counter asked if we needed a shuttle.

"Nope, we can walk," Pash said. We argued all the way to the airport terminal.

"What if I had wanted a shuttle?" I said.

"Well, you should have said something," she replied.

"You never give me a chance; you just make all the decisions."

"Someone really is grumpy," she chided. "It's okay, you'll feel better after the walk. It will wake you up!"

I rolled my eyes as we got our tickets and headed to the gate to board the plane.

"Ladye, I was thinking we should start flying first class because we're in a different tax bracket now, and we need to let the people know how we shine," Pash said.

"You can fly first class but book me in coach. This ride is just over two hours long, and I'm not paying double the price to sit in the front of a damn airplane to go to the same destination as the person four rows behind me. We're only on the plane for a short time, so it's a no for me! I hate wasting money on dumb shit."

"Okay, damn, I give up! I was just saying we're different now, and we should splurge one time in our lives," Pash sighed.

"We will, I promise you, but not this time," I said, softening my voice. I held her hand and leaned against her. "You're right; we do deserve to be treated like royalty. It's just that as soon as we blink, we'll be there, so it's not worth it. But our time is coming."

Pash grinned and gave me a hug. We boarded the plane, and while we waited for the captain to announce we were clear for takeoff, I whispered a little prayer.

"Next stop, Houston, Texas. God, watch over us on this flight! Amen!"

Reem Denise

Chapter Twelve

It was quite a change from Cincinnati's brisk 60-degree weather to Houston's 85 degrees of pure sun. I sighed happily and looked around at the beautiful park, with its luscious trees and green grass. The day was especially wonderful because of my companion who sat next to me on the bench. We had been chilling and talking for the last 20 minutes when suddenly Jayson (Jay for short) fell silent.

I wondered what he was thinking about when it hit me: I finally figured out why I was so attracted to this man. It was his presence. His aura. Something about him made me want to do things I'd never even imagined doing. Just sitting next to him, barely touching, made me want him so much. And apparently, he felt the same, because I could see his manhood straining against his pants. So, what was a woman supposed to do about a thing like that? I looked around to make sure no one was watching and placed my hand on his rod. A smile spread across his face as it pulsed against my hand, getting bigger and harder. It felt like bliss. I wanted him more than he could possibly know.

Jay was big, black, bald, and sexy. When he spoke, his voice was deep and low, almost like Barry White mixed with Billy Dee Williams. Usually, he was dressed in a suit, but today he was cute and casual in a black and white Coogi shirt, black shorts, and white Air Jordans. He was smoking a Black & Mild cigar, with a toothpick resting in his left ear. His teeth were perfect, and I loved his smile. When he worked at the club, he was so serious, with a mean scowl created to keep people in line. But when he smiled, his whole face came alive, and his eyes twinkled.

The connection of his mustache and beard really accentuated his mouth, and when he French kissed me, I felt like a girl putting on a new pair of jeans and finding the fit to be perfect.

He continued to smoke, rubbing my back gently and not saying a word, just making me think about him. I think he's doing it on purpose! He knows I want him.

"I miss you," he whispered in my ear as he kissed my neck.

"Well, I'm here now," I said breathlessly.

"I want you to feel me." He kept kissing my neck and licked my ear passionately. Heaven knows I wanted to feel him. It had been a whole month since I felt that big, black shaft in my fat wetness. We became lost in anticipation of what was to come when we suddenly realized we weren't alone.

A lady walked by with her two barking dogs and ruined the whole damn moment! Bitch! We quickly let go of each other and scooted apart as kids began to fill up the nearby playground, forcing us to behave ourselves.

"Hey, baby, I have a poem for you," Jay said.

"Oh! Where is it?"

"In my head, sweetness. I wrote it for you." As he recited the poem, titled "Beautiful Chanelle," I couldn't help but wonder about his intentions. This man must really love me! I hadn't expected such a romantic interlude.

Just as he finished, four boys walked past us on their way to the basketball court to get a game going. Jay pulled me closer and kissed me with such force that I instantly became wet and filled with lust. The surprised look on my face must have been comical. I think he just did that because one of the boys spoke to me and smiled. Jealous much?

"Baby, I have to make a call, and I left my phone in your truck," I said, regretting that we had to come up for air. We walked back to the truck, where he opened the passenger door and helped me in. The person I was calling wasn't answering, so I checked through my messages, a little irritated that I was being ignored. Don't worry about it. He'll call. For now, I'm Chanelle, and I'm in Houston.

I turned my attention to Jay, who was leaning back and listening to music. His eyes were closed, and I thought he might have fallen asleep until I felt him breathing on my neck.

"Take your panties off," Jay whispered in my ear, nibbling on it.

"No! People can see us!" I hesitated.

"That's the thrill of it, my sexy queen." He slid my dress up and rubbed my thigh. Reluctantly, I took off my pink silk panties and, with sudden rebelliousness, hung them around the rearview mirror.

"Oh, I like that." Jay put his hand under my dress and twirled his fingers around inside me.

"Girl, you are so wet!"

"Jay, stop!" I begged, but I couldn't help grinding on his fingers because they felt so good inside me. "Please... stop..."

"I will not," he said in his low, deep voice. He lifted my dress slightly above my waist and bent down to drink from the honeypot, savoring every drop of my lust and not missing a single one. Oh my gosh, pure pleasure!

"Jayson, please stop! People are staring!" I glanced over at the car next to us, where a man and woman had their arms around each other as they watched us. They were engaged in their own sex play, and our actions seemed to inspire them.

Jay looked over at them and grinned. "They're welcome to watch," he said. He leaned back in his seat and unzipped his pants, revealing his purple boxers. Taking my hand, he placed it on his throbbing manhood.

"I want to see it; I haven't seen it in a while," I said, biting my bottom lip. He pulled the tip of his rod out, and I licked it softly, which prompted him to pull down his boxers and take it out completely. I licked, sucked, moaned, and slobbered all over it. He let out a groan, and I hummed a little song, just for a moment, so he could feel the vibration.

"That's just a sample for now; a taste of what's to come," I teased.

"Sit on the armrest," he commanded, and I always do what I'm told. He lifted my dress again and devoured my wetness like it was a candy shop. As he slurped my sugar walls, all I could do was moan. My slit felt incredible; it was jumping, rolling, and vibrating all at the same time. I thought my body was going to explode, and my head might spin right off. I'd never felt anything like it.

"Don't stop, please!" I whimpered. Jay paused and looked up at me mischievously before diving right back in. I snickered when I heard the couple in the next car moaning. What had started as a lover's lane was really happening until a car pulled up on the other side of us. The woman frowned at our steamed-up windows, and when she realized her husband was trying to get a good look, she hit him.

We stopped what we were doing and burst out laughing. Who would have ever thought a trip to the park could be so much fun? I couldn't wait until later, so we could really get together and handle our business.

When we pulled up to the curb at Pash's apartment, it was raining cats and dogs, so we stayed in the truck and made out. His tongue filled my mouth completely, and he tasted so sweet. We kissed so much and for so long that we didn't even notice when the rain stopped.

"You wanna go back to the park and try again?" Jay smiled deviously, playing with my underwear that were still hanging from the mirror.

"We can!" I didn't hesitate this time.

When we got there, we decided to back the truck in so the front was facing the park. That way, no one could see what we were doing because nothing was behind us but trees and a wall. We let the seats down, transforming his eight-passenger vehicle into a pick-up truck, and locked the doors just to be safe. We hopped in the back, and Jay closed the trunk with the remote. I pulled up my dress, he took out his manhood, and we fucked like nobody's business.

"You have to keep watching to make sure nobody parks next to us," I mumbled between heavy breaths. He entered me, and I felt his rod going deep. I moved my hips in rhythm with his; my sopping wetness screamed with delight. We both closed our eyes and imagined it never ending. When we opened them at the same time, it was synchronic as our gazes met. It all came back to me why I loved him so much.

My mound throbbed as he stroked it, and I felt myself about to climax. I tried to control it, but the intensity was overwhelming. He must have felt my body quivering because his rod responded. I grabbed his ass to make him go deeper, and suddenly we both climaxed. It was a long, drawn-out, almost torturous release, and we both moaned with ecstasy and satisfaction.

Looking up at that handsome man, I traced his face with my fingers and sighed happily. "Damn," I said softly. "I can't wait until tonight!"

Chapter Thirteen

As night fell, I waited anxiously for Jay to text me. I tried not to think about it, but I couldn't go more than a couple of minutes before I checked my phone. Maybe I accidentally muted it. Maybe he texted, and I didn't hear it. I should check my volume.

I sat cross-legged on the couch in Pash's apartment, bent over, looking at my phone like it was a scientific experiment that could cure cancer. Finally, after making sure all the settings were right, I put the damn thing down on the coffee table.

Thirty seconds later, I heard the double ping my text messaging makes. I grinned, thinking I'd wait a few minutes before I looked. Make him wait, that's what I'll do. But my impatient ass won the battle, and I snatched up my cell. Smiling, I expected to see something from Jayson, but it was some random guy I'd talked to in the club once.

"Hey, it's Ryan. I miss you."

"Who?" Who the hell is Ryan?

"I met you last month when you were dancing. I was the handsome one in the purple shirt."

I barely remembered meeting anyone like that. Obviously, he wasn't memorable. But I got a lot of that as a dancer. Men were always fascinated by me and wanted to "get to know me better." Unfortunately for them, I was rarely impressed by any of the clientele. I was just doing my job and raking in the money.

"Riddle me this: How did you get my number? Considering I don't give my number out and don't remember you, what do you want?" I took my time sending him the message, then put the phone back down.

Memoirs of an Invisible Woman

A couple of minutes later, I got another notification. It's gotta be Jay! I picked up my cell and saw a picture of a dick. And it obviously wasn't Jay's. I sent several laughing emojis. Maybe that'll bring him down a notch or two. It was a nice dick, but it didn't make me wet. It just irritated me that he would have the audacity to send the picture when we didn't know each other. So I lit into him.

"Listen, my dude, don't send me pics of your dick! I've seen everything from the smallest to the biggest, so that shit doesn't make me want to fuck you at all! Who the hell do you think you are?"

"I apologize, my queen. I just really want to get to know you."

Oh my god. I blocked him and deleted his messages, including the photo. Why should I waste my time on a man like that?

I heard another ping and sighed, thinking my block didn't work. But it was Jay.

"I want you."

"Oh really?" I answered. "How bad?"

"I can't stand it. I'm going to die if I don't get a taste of that fine wet wet soon!"

"Well, all good things have to wait," I wrote. "Are we still on for tonight?" Don't you dare let me down.

"I wouldn't miss it for anything. Just getting the girls ready so I can drop them off at their mom's."

"Okay, well let me know when you're done."

"I will. Keep it wet for me, baby."

As I sat there grinning like a fool, Pash walked in the door. She stopped in the middle of the living room, and we looked at each other awkwardly. Then we both laughed nervously.

"I don't know whether to ask you questions about your day or mind my own business, which is very hard for me to do—you know that," she said. "But I'm also tired as hell. I've been in meetings all day at work, and I'm so exhausted. I just need a nice hot shower."

"It's all good," I said. "Go up and take your shower; take your time. I'll fix you a drink in a bit, and we'll talk if we're both up for it."

She didn't argue about that and walked into her bedroom. I hopped on Facebook to see what the rest of the world was doing and messed around for about an hour, just being nosy. And it was fun to judge. People always put their best stuff on social media when we know it isn't all caviar and parties like they want us to believe.

My BFF and I sat at the kitchen table and talked about the shit we were going through.

"Pash, I'm really torn between two men. There's the one at home that I am in love with, my best friend, the one I want to marry and grow old with. With him, I know security is guaranteed, but he is so boring and never wants to do anything. Then there's the man who lives here, who makes me feel like my world is all he cares about and makes me feel good as hell. Both of their sex is off the chain. I don't worry about either one of them in that area. They both have baggage, but who doesn't nowadays? I'm just so confused." I shook my head, trying to clear my mind.

"Girl, you're gonna have to do what's best for you and only you at the end of the day. And sorry, beautiful, but you're the only one who can make this decision," Pash said, as she always does. That's why I love her. She'll give me advice when I need it, even if I don't want it, and she knows when to tell me to shut up and quit bitching. She's silly as hell, but when I need her, she's there in a heartbeat. She always has my back, even if I don't follow her advice. I cherish her, and we respect each other's boundaries. Friends like that don't come around often.

"L, I have a question for you, and be completely honest with me, because this is something you really need to figure out," Pash smirked at me.

"What, bitch? Just ask the gotdamn question then," I said, folding my arms and crossing my legs.

"Are you ever going to tell Jayson your real name?" she smiled sarcastically.

"Not anytime soon, because one world isn't going to meet the other. So probably not for a while, honestly." Now Pash had me thinking about it. Should I? Hell, no! I absolutely should not!

Reem Denise

Chapter Fourteen

I put the finishing touches on my outfit and was practically glowing as I anticipated my evening with Jay. I was working that night, but my fine bodyguard would be there every step of the way.

I checked my lipstick, put on my big hoop earrings, and dabbed a little Chanel behind my ears. I twirled in front of the full-length mirror, nodding with admiration. You can't go wrong with a classic black dress. It hugged my body in all the right places and accentuated my toned legs. I had my dance outfits hung up nicely in garment bags and would change in the club dressing room. Just as I bent over to put my stilettos on, my cell phone rang. Guess he's having a hard time keeping his pants on.

"Hey, Mr. Impatient," I said breathlessly.

"Call me on my cell phone," a voice that wasn't Jay said.

"Who is this?" I asked.

"Who the hell do you think? And who's impatient? Who were you expecting?"

Uh oh. Play it cool. "Hold on, Julian. I'll call back." I heard the phone at the other end slam down.

I called Julian's cell, and he answered on the first ring.

"What's up?" I asked.

"Nothing."

"Well, I've been blowing up your phone since six, and you haven't picked up, but I'm not going to start with you; it's whatever."

"Ladye, don't start that shit! I told you that it was my daughter's birthday, and I was over there giving her a party, so what now?" he growled.

"What the fuck ever! You didn't tell me it was her birthday!" I yelled. "But what the fuck does that have to do with you answering the gotdamn phone? Every time you're around your kids' mother, you act like you can't answer the phone like you're still fucking her or something. But whatever, like I said!"

"What do you want me to do, Ladye? Answer the phone and tell you that I'm over there with my kids?"

"Hell yeah! That's exactly what I want you to do! Answer the fucking phone and say exactly that, unless you have something to hide, my nigga."

Julian was quiet for a couple of minutes, and I heard him sigh. "No, I don't have anything to hide. I just didn't think you would want to hear that I'm over at my baby mama's house."

This man was trying my last nerves. Where did he get off assuming what my reaction would be? This lack of communication was going to have to stop if I had anything to say about it.

"Why the fuck would I care if you're doing something with your kids? They are your kids, and if that's all it is, you shouldn't have a problem telling me that!" I shot back.

"Ladye, I didn't want you to call me so we could argue. I just wanted to see how your trip was going. So, how's it going?" he asked.

I took a deep breath and tried to calm down. "My trip is cool. I'm just resting and getting my thoughts together. Wondering what the hell you're up to."

Pash stuck her head out of her bedroom. "Goodnight, girl!" She saw me on the phone and mouthed *sorry*.

"Night, Pash! See you in the morning!" It was good that Julian knew I was at her house. I waved to her from the couch.

"I might not work tomorrow!" she yelled.

"Okay, that's cool," I laughed.

I started right back with Julian, not missing a beat. "Well, all I know is that I think you're still fucking your kids' mother, Julian. And it's all good though."

"Ladye, what are you talking about?"

I came at him again. "Just what I said, mutha fucka, but who cares?"

"Ladye, I'm not fucking her, but I do go see my kids every day, and that's not going to stop!" Julian was starting to get fed up with me, and I could hear it in his voice.

"I don't expect you to. If you didn't, you would be less than a man. Julian, I told you what I want, but you seem to have a problem giving it to me, like something is holding you back. To be honest, I'm starting to get tired of it!"

"You tired of what, Ladye? Tired of me taking care of you? Tired of me paying all your fucking bills? Tired of me taking care of your fucking kids? What the fuck you tired of? Please fucking tell me!" Julian roared. Obviously, I struck a nerve.

"Julian, I'm not going back and forth with you no more!" I shouted.

"First of all, lower your fucking voice before I fly down there and choke the shit out of you! I'm a fucking man, and you're going to start respecting me, or you'll be by your fucking self! I promise you that! Now, you don't want to argue because you know I take care of you, and you don't want that fucking well to run dry! You materialistic ass brat! You're really starting to piss me off, and I'm getting tired of this shit every time I go see my fucking kids! You and Sam can go fuck yourselves! I'm sick of both you bitches!" Julian hung up the phone.

Pash came out of her bedroom in her robe. "What's with all the yellin'?"

"I was talking to Julian. This nigga just hung up on me!" I paced in front of the couch, waving my arms.

"Oh no, he didn't! Whatcha gonna do, girl?"

"I swear if I didn't have a shift at the club in 30 minutes, I would hop my ass right back on a plane and go smack the shit out of him! Fucking idiot!"

"Why did he get so mad?" she asked.

"Okay, the conversation was getting heated, but that's no reason to hang up in my face. Not to mention he knows I hate that shit. It's all good, though; I bet he calls me way before I call his bitch ass!"

"You know it, girl!"

"Stupid dumb fuck! Oh, I'm so pissed. Let me clear my head so I can go get this money! I'll deal with Julian's ass later."

As I sat in the room waiting for Jay to call me so I could get this night over and done with, I had Alicia Keys playing in the background. It was only 9:00 PM, and it was so dark outside when I looked out the window that I could hardly see the parking lot. Why the hell don't they have more lighting in this damn lot? The shit looks like a scary movie scene or something.

I heard my phone vibrating on the bed. I reached over to grab it and looked at the number; it was a 716-area code. There's only one person I know with that area code.

"Hello," I answered the phone with a huge smile on my face, ready to have a full-blown conversation.

"Ladye, what's up, baby girl?" the voice on the other end replied.

"What's good, Knight? Long time no hear. Where you been, homie? I haven't heard your voice in forever," I let out a small laugh.

"Shid, you know me, mommy. I'm just taking care of business, movin' and shakin', stayin' out the way, you know—nigga shit," Knight started to laugh.

Now, Knight was this dude I met years ago in high school. He was from Buffalo, NY, but came to Ohio to live with his grandparents for a few years, so we ended up going to the same school since we all lived on the same street. Knight was fine as hell; he was about 6'2", with high yellow skin and this curly-ass black hair that was thick and pretty. His eyes were so bright, and his long eyelashes made his eyes look even better. Why do guys always get the best eyelashes? His nose was slender, and he had nice, kiss-me-all-the-time lips. Knight's frame was narrow and lanky, and he walked with such confidence—always a ten out of ten—with a very mellow-toned voice.

"Knight," I broke my train of thought. "What's good with you? I don't even know the last time I heard from you. What do you need from me?" I was a little curious because this call was literally out of nowhere.

"Shid, Ma, you crossed my mind, and I said let me call Ms. Ladye and see if her number is still the same. The fact that you still have the same number you had in high school is crazy as hell to me," he laughed.

"Knight, I suck my teeth and roll my eyes. Now you know I'm about to call bullshit! Because the last time I heard from you, you said you didn't ever want to talk to me again because I wouldn't choose you over Corey. Then I got with Julian, and you were really pissed then, so stop playing with me and tell me what you need!"

I could hear Knight take a deep breath. "Ladye, that shit is old, and you know I always kept up with you over the years. I see you have a beautiful family, and your careers are taking off. Shiiiid, you are a hot commodity in the town," he laughed sarcastically.

"Knight, what the hell do you mean, careers? I only have one career. What did I miss?" I asked because now I was getting suspicious.

"No, ma, that's what I mean. Your salon is having you travel all around the world doing shows and shit. You know I travel a lot too because of my investments. I have to travel all around the world, and you'd be surprised at what I've seen on my adventures," he laughed again.

"Knight, is there something you want to ask me or tell me? Because it seems like you're talking in riddles, and I'm pressed for time, and my patience is running really low."

"Ladye, my reason for calling you seriously is to ask you, have you seen your brother Petey? These niggas in town are looking for him because they say he owes some people some money."

"Knight, boy, what money would my brother owe to anyone in our town that I haven't heard about? Anything that has to do with my family, I know about. Now you say Petey owes people money? Well, how much money are we talking? And please give me exact numbers and names."

I could hear Knight pausing like he was calculating some shit. "Well, Ladye, my love, he owes me $10,548.63 to be exact, that's with interest and late fees," Knight laughed.

"I know you're fucking lying! Why would he owe you so much money?" I was pissed because I knew what type of street shit Knight was on, and to know my stupid ass brother got caught up in some shit without coming to me was crazy!

"Ladye, I'm only giving you a courtesy call because one: I love you, and two: I don't want this to get ugly with your brother. He keeps dodging me, and this shit has been going on for two months now. I'm never going to go to your parents' house because I respect them too much, but Petey needs to pay me my money, or this shit's gonna get real ugly."

Now I could hear the tone of Knight's voice, and I knew he was not playing. This shit was real.

"Knight, I'll be home Monday, and if you can just hold off until then, I will give you the money with no problem, I promise. Knight, please don't do anything to Petey that would kill my parents. Not to mention it's going to jack my heart up; I mean, he is my twin, and we feel a lot of the same shit. Knight, please let me fix this."

"Ladye, because it's you, I'm going to hold off until Monday, but just know you owe me big time for this, and I will be coming to collect," Knight laughed.

"I'm pretty sure you will, Knight. Talk to you soon." I hung up the phone.

I'm going to fucking kill Petey. His stupid ass always gets me into some shit because of his poor decision-making. This is the third time I've had to save him, and now I gotta take money out of my funds to pay off another one of his fucking mess-ups. Petey knows that if I find out about it, I'm always going to bail his ass out because he's my younger brother by eight minutes, but he's my parents' only son. The girls always take care of him, and he doesn't mind putting us in fucked-up positions. I have a strange feeling this is not going to be the last of Petey's shit!

I got the text from Jay telling me he was outside in his truck. Grabbing my purse and outfits, I checked myself in the mirror, making sure I didn't look as angry as I felt. Suddenly, I got the strangest sensation and froze, staring at the face looking back at me. Who is this woman? What does she want? What is she doing with her life? Something inside told me to pay attention to these

"I know you're fucking lying! Why would he owe you so much money?" I was pissed because I knew what type of street shit Knight was on, and to know my stupid ass brother got caught up in some shit without coming to me was crazy!

"Ladye, I'm only giving you a courtesy call because one: I love you, and two: I don't want this to get ugly with your brother. He keeps dodging me, and this shit has been going on for two months now. I'm never going to go to your parents' house because I respect them too much, but Petey needs to pay me my money, or this shit's gonna get real ugly."

Now I could hear the tone of Knight's voice, and I knew he was not playing. This shit was real.

"Knight, I'll be home Monday, and if you can just hold off until then, I will give you the money with no problem, I promise. Knight, please don't do anything to Petey that would kill my parents. Not to mention it's going to jack my heart up; I mean, he is my twin, and we feel a lot of the same shit. Knight, please let me fix this."

"Ladye, because it's you, I'm going to hold off until Monday, but just know you owe me big time for this, and I will be coming to collect," Knight laughed.

"I'm pretty sure you will, Knight. Talk to you soon." I hung up the phone.

I'm going to fucking kill Petey. His stupid ass always gets me into some shit because of his poor decision-making. This is the third time I've had to save him, and now I gotta take money out of my funds to pay off another one of his fucking mess-ups. Petey knows that if I find out about it, I'm always going to bail his ass out because he's my younger brother by eight minutes, but he's my parents' only son. The girls always take care of him, and he doesn't mind putting us in fucked-up positions. I have a strange feeling this is not going to be the last of Petey's shit!

I got the text from Jay telling me he was outside in his truck. Grabbing my purse and outfits, I checked myself in the mirror, making sure I didn't look as angry as I felt. Suddenly, I got the strangest sensation and froze, staring at the face looking back at me. Who is this woman? What does she want? What is she doing with her life? Something inside told me to pay attention to these questions. I took a deep breath and looked around. That was weird. Okay, Ladye, get a hold of yourself. You've been watching too much TV or something. I tried to shake off the doomsday feelings, but somehow it felt like a premonition. I knew deep in my soul that things were about to get crazy.

Reem Denise

Chapter Fifteen

The drive to Club Cheetahs was long and silent. What usually was a twenty-minute ride felt like two hours. I heard "Secret Garden" by Quincy Jones playing, but it seemed distant. Why can't I shake this feeling I have?

"You okay, baby?" Jay asked.

"Yes, I'm fine. I just feel a little uneasy, like something is wrong or something is going to happen. I've only ever had this feeling one other time in my life, and that's when... you know what, never mind. Let me get my head together so I can get this money and do my job," I smirked as I grabbed Jay's free hand. "Thank you for always being my peace. I love that you want the best for me, regardless." Jay kissed my hand, and we held hands until we got to the club.

The club was packed—I mean, it looked like a thousand cars were out there, and the line wrapped around the corner.

"Why is it so crowded?" I asked Jay.

"I guess niggas heard you were back in town and want to see what you've got up your sleeve, or should I say thong?" he laughed.

"Really, Jayson? Ha ha, very funny," I giggled.

"I'm going to let you go in the back entrance. Wait for me to park the truck, and I'll walk you to the dressing room," he said. "I'll call Charlie and let him know you're in the building. You know he's got to come and talk his shit as usual and figure out how he can get you here full-time. Even though you tell him every time it's not happening, he still has to try."

Jay let me out of the truck, and I waited as instructed in the hallway. When we walked down the hallway together, it felt like the Walk of Shame. I really couldn't shake the bad feeling; I felt like I was about to have a panic attack.

"Chanelle, are you good? You're sweating like crazy! Do you want to leave? You don't look good!" Jay's face was full of worry.

"No, I'm fine, just hot. Once I get to my dressing room, I'll get some water and wine to calm my nerves down."

As I opened the dressing room door, I saw roses everywhere—literally fifteen dozen. I couldn't even see my vanity.

"Who sent all these damn flowers? Now I'm aggravated. Jay! Really, all these flowers? Are you kidding me?"

I tried to find somewhere to lay my costumes down, but there were flowers everywhere.

"I definitely didn't send these," Jay said. "I mean, this is overkill!"

"Okay, if you didn't, then who did?" Oh my God. A flashback of Thursday in the salon came to mind, but it couldn't be the same person. "My worlds don't mix! Nobody knows me here that would know me back home. This is a sick game, and I am not playing it."

Jay found a card among one of the bunches. "From your Secret Admirer, not Jay or Julian!" he read. "Who the fuck is Julian?"

"Wait, what?" I looked nervously back at him. "I don't know who Julian is. These flowers can't possibly be for me!" I continued to look around, then I saw another card.

"I'll follow you wherever you go, my beautiful Chanelle."

Oh shit, it is the same person from back home, and whoever it is knows both of my identities. Now I was scared, but I had to play it off.

"Listen, Jay, I don't know who is sending me flowers or why I'm being stalked. I don't mess with anyone else; you are the only man I want!" I tried to hug him, but he pushed me away.

"Baby, just get ready. I'll be outside your door watching. Knock when you're ready to go upstairs." He kissed my forehead and walked out the door.

Dammit, now I'm up shit's creek without a paddle. It was obvious that he knew something was off. He had never questioned me before because he never had to, but now I felt like questions were about to start, and I was a horrible liar. I could hide stuff, but lying when I was asked questions was totally different.

As I laid my head on my vanity to channel my thoughts, my phone rang.

"Hey, Ladye, it's Mina!"

"Mina, what's wrong? You never call me Ladye when you know I'm out of town, nor do you call me this late!"

"Ladye, are you coming home tomorrow or Monday?" She sounded very weird and off.

"Why, Mina? What's wrong?"

"I just need to know."

"When do you need me home, sis?" I asked.

"If you could please come home tomorrow," she cried.

"Mina, what's wrong? What happened? Just tell me, please?"

"Ladye, just come home, please." She was crying even harder.

"Dammit, Mina, what the fuck is wrong? You are starting to piss me off because I know something happened! I'll be on the first flight, but what is wrong?"

"Ladye, somebody shot Dad and Petey." Her voice was trembling. "Ladye, please sit down before I keep talking."

"Mina, what the fuck else? Please just tell me!" I could feel my tears about to flow down my face.

"Corey!" Mina cried. "Corey is in the hospital; she needs you ASAP!"

I dropped my phone, the sound of it hitting the floor drowned out by the roar of panic in my ears. My heart raced, and my breaths quickened as I fought to process Mina's words. Somebody shot Dad and Petey. The weight of those words crashed down on me, and I felt like the ground was slipping beneath my feet.

"Ladye, please, you have to come home now," Mina pleaded, her voice breaking. "I don't know what's going to happen, but we need you!"

I stumbled back, leaning against the vanity, the overwhelming scent of roses twisting into a suffocating fog. How could this be happening? My life had just begun to feel stable again, and now it was unraveling before my eyes.

"Hold on, Mina. I'll be there as fast as I can," I managed to choke out, my mind racing. I thought of Jay, of the flowers and the secret admirer, everything felt like a cruel joke. Was this all connected? Had whoever been stalking me finally made a move, or was this just a coincidence?

I grabbed my purse, my hands shaking as I fumbled to find my keys. The weight of my brother's reckless choices loomed over me, and I couldn't shake the feeling that this was my fault. I had always been there to bail him out, but this time, it felt like it was too late.

"Chanelle!" Jay's voice echoed down the hall, pulling me from my thoughts. "You ready?"

"No! I can't! I have to go home," I shouted, my voice cracking. "Something happened to my family!"

"What? What do you mean?" He rushed into the room, confusion etched on his face, but I could see the alarm in his eyes.

"Just... just let me go!" I screamed, my heart racing as I made a move for the door.

Jay stepped in front of me, concern and fear flashing in his gaze. "You're not going alone. I'm coming with you."

"Jay, you don't understand! I can't have you involved in this—"

"I don't care," he interrupted, his voice firm. "You need someone with you. We'll figure it out together."

I stared at him, torn between the desire to protect him and the need for his support. But deep down, I knew I couldn't face whatever awaited me alone.

Suddenly, my phone buzzed on the floor, and I dropped down to grab it. It was a message from an unknown number. My heart raced as I opened it:

"You thought you could escape the past, but it's coming for you. Be careful who you trust."

I felt a chill race down my spine. This was the same person from before, the one who knew both of my lives.

"Ladye, let's go!" Jay urged again, grabbing my hand and pulling me up.

Reem Denise

As we rushed out of the dressing room, I cast one last glance at the roses—symbolic of the beauty that had quickly turned to thorns. My heart pounded as I stepped out into the chaos of the club, uncertainty swirling around me.

Whatever awaited me back home—whatever dark truths lay hidden—I wasn't sure my fragile façade could hold up beneath it.

And as I stepped into the night, a sense of foreboding loomed in the air, like a storm about to break. I took a deep breath, ready to confront the impending danger, knowing that I had to uncover the truth before it swallowed me whole.

Acknowledgments

There are a few people I want to acknowledge who helped me make this vision come to pass and who listened to my ideas, giving me constructive criticism throughout this whole process.

First, I really want to say thank you, God! A lot of people will ask, "How can you thank God when you're writing an adult book?" I'll say this: God gave me an amazing ability to write and see things from a different perspective, and for that, I say thank you, God! He never left me, even when I felt like giving up on Him and throwing in the towel, so once again, thank you, God! I will never stop thanking Him for His many blessings.

I want to thank my mom, dad, and stepmom (aka Stuff), for teaching me no matter what quitting is not an option. To always try to do my best no matter what the circumstances and to be the best version of me so that way no one can ever say I wasn't a genuine person.

Mom, thank you for your pure heart and loving me no matter what. You showed me how to be a woman of God.

Dad, thank you for your endless talks of right from wrong. Thank you for being my first example of what a man should be to his children.

To my stepmom Stuff, thank you for being a second mom to me and always treating me like you would your own child. Thank you for showing me that it's okay to love a stepmom and for always being there for me no matter what. Even in my older age, I still truly love my stepmom so much.

I also want to thank Pastor Bertha Brinson and the late Bishop Joseph Brinson Jr., who have been my Mom and Dad in the Gospel for many years now. They taught me to keep going no matter what the doubters say and showed me Kingdom love and the unconditional love of Jesus Christ. I just wish Bishop was here to see me finally step out on faith and not be scared anymore, but I know he's watching and smiling down on me. Pastor Bertha, you are my hero; you have talked me through so many dark times and prayed for me when I didn't even know I needed prayer. I love you, Lady B!

Thank you also to Bishop Fred D. Gooden III and Lady Jameliah Gooden for being my leaders and guiding me to the next level in my spiritual journey. Thank you for your countless teachings and words spoken over me. I love you both so much!

To all my family and friends: I love you all so much, and I couldn't do this without y'all! Family and friends are so important, and I thank God for my village.

To my daughter Tyra Handley, thank you for listening to my idea for my book cover and being so patient with your mom—I know I worked your nerve, but hey, that's what moms are for! I also want to acknowledge my niece Shalisa, who listened to my craziness all night sometimes.

Next, let me thank my editor and typesetter, Abbrielle Artrip, owner of Dove and Quill Editing LLC. Thank you for helping me put everything together and being a prayer warrior for me. You stood in the gap for me, and I appreciate it so much.

Last but not least, to my Julian (he knows who he is)—thank you for all these years of friendship and love; you make me stronger than you know.

Photo courtesy of the author

Reem Denise is an emerging author of adult fiction, debuting with a novel rooted in the rich, complex life of Buffalo, New York. Inspired by personal experiences, she crafts stories full of depth, emotion, and authenticity. A proud mother of five, Reem balances her love for writing with a passion for DIY projects, finding creativity in every part of life. Now living in North Carolina, she continues to draw from her Buffalo roots to shape her work. Her debut novel marks the start of an exciting literary journey she's eager to share with readers everywhere.

Made in the USA
Columbia, SC
05 January 2025